7 BILLION LIVES ARE IN DANGER.
13 STRANGERS WITH TERRIFYING NIGHTMARES.
1 ENEMY WILL STOP AT NOTHING TO DESTROY US ALL.

MY NAME IS SAM.
I AM ONE OF THE LAST THIRTEEN.
OUR BATTLE CONTINUES . . .

# For Nicole, for always being there—JP.

Scholastic Canada Ltd.
604 King Street West, Toronto, Ontario M5V 1E1, Canada

Scholastic Inc.
557 Broadway, New York, NY 10012, USA

Scholastic Australia Pty Limited
PO Box 579, Gosford, NSW 2250, Australia

Scholastic New Zealand Limited
Private Bag 94407, Botany, Manukau 2163, New Zealand

Scholastic Children's Books
Euston House, 24 Eversholt Street, London NW1 1DB, UK

www.scholastic.ca

Library and Archives Canada Cataloguing in Publication
Phelan, James, 1979-
        12 / by James Phelan.

(The last thirteen)
ISBN 978-1-4431-2483-6

        I. Title. II. Title: Twelve. III. Series: Phelan, James, 1979-
Last thirteen.

PZ7.P52Tw 2013          j823'.92          C2013-901802-6

First published by Scholastic Australia in 2013. This edition published by Scholastic Canada Ltd. In 2014.
Text copyright © 2013 by James Phelan. Illustrations & design copyright © 2013 by Scholastic Australia.
Illustrations by Chad Mitchell. Design by Nicole Stofberg.

Cover photography: Blueprint © istockphoto.com/Adam Korzekwa; Parkour Tic-Tac © istockphoto.com/Willie B. Thomas; Climbing wall © istockphoto.com/microgen; Leonardo da Vinci (Sepia) © istockphoto.com/pictore; Gears © istockphoto.com/-Oxford-; Mechanical blueprint © istockphoto.com/teekid; Circuit board © istockphoto.com/Björn Meyer; Map © istockphoto.com/alengo; Grunge drawing © istockphoto.com/aleksandar velasevic; World map © istockphoto.com/Maksim Pasko; Internet © istockphoto.com/Andrey Prokhorov; Inside clock © istockphoto.com/LdF; Space galaxy © istockphoto.com/Sergii Tsololo; Sunset © istockphoto.com/Joakim Leroy; Blue flare © istockphoto.com/YouraPechkin; Global communication © istockphoto.com/chadive samanthakamani; Earth satellites © istockphoto.com/Alexey Popov; Girl portrait © istockphoto.com/peter zelei; Student & board © istockphoto.com/zhang bo; Young man serious © istockphoto.com/Jacob Wackerhausen; Portrait man © istockphoto.com/Alina Solovyova-Vincent; Sad expression © istockphoto.com/Shelly Perry; Content man © istockphoto.com/drbimages; Pensive man © istockphoto.com/Chuck Schmidt; Black and pink © istockphoto.com/blackwaterimages; Punk Girl © istockphoto.com/Kuzma; Woman escaping © Jose antonio Sanchez reyes/Photos.com; Young running man © Tatiana Belova/Photos.com; Gears clock © Jupiterimages/Photos.com; Woman portrait © Nuzza/Shutterstock; Explosions © Leigh Prather/Dreamstime.com; Landscape blueprints © Firebrandphotography/Dreamstime.com; Jump over wall © Ammentorp/Dreamstime.com; Mountains, CAN © Akadiusz Iwanicki/Dreamstime.com; Sphinx Bucegi © Adrian Nicolae/Dreamstime.com; Big mountains © Hoptrop/Dreamstime.com; Sunset mountains © Pklimenko/Dreamstime.com; Mountains lake © Jan Mika/Dreamstime.com; Blue night sky © Mack2happy/Dreamstime.com; Old writing © Empire331/Dreamstime.com; Young man © Shuen Ho Wang/Dreamstime.com; Abstract cells © Sur/Dreamstime.com; Helicopter © Evren Kalinbacak/Dreamstime.com; Aeroplane © Rgbe/Dreamstime.com; Phrenology illustration © Mcarrel/Dreamstime.com; Abstract interior © Sur/Dreamstime.com; Papyrus © Cebreros/Dreamstime.com; Blue shades © Mohamed Osama/Dreamstime.com; Blue background © Matusciac/Dreamstime.com; Sphinx and Pyramid © Dan Breckwoldt/Dreamstime.com; Blue background2 © Cammeraydave/Dreamstime.com; Abstract shapes © Lisa Mckown/Dreamstime.com; Yellow Field © Simon Greig/Dreamstime.com; Blue background3 © Sergey Skrebnev/Dreamstime.com; Blue eye © Richard Thomas/Dreamstime.com; Abstract landscape © Crazy80frog/Dreamstime.com; Rameses II © Jose I. Soto/Dreamstime.com; Helicopter © Sculpies/Dreamstime.com; Vitruvian man © Cornelius20/Dreamstime.com; Scarab beetle © Charon/Dreamstime.com; Eye of Horus © Charon/Dreamstime.com; Handsome male portrait © DigitalHand Studio/Shutterstock.com; Teen girl © CREATISTA/Shutterstock.com; Rome sunset © istockphoto.com/fotoVoyager; Postcards from Italy (series) © Knud Nielsen/Dreamstime.com; Dark tunnel © istockphoto.com/peeterv; Juliet's balcony © istockphoto.com/massimofusaro; Napoli Piazza del Plebiscito © istockphoto.com/bbuong; Compass and ancient map of Italy © Travelling-light/Dreamstime.com; Carnival mask © Melinda Nagy/Dreamstime.com; Trevi Fountain © istockphoto.com/traveler1116; Bernini's Colonnade © istockphoto.com/compassandcamera; Pantheon © istockphoto.com/DNY59; Rome © istockphoto.com/spooh; Holy Door, St Peter's Basilica © istockphoto.com/markgoddard; Map of Italy © istockphoto.com/Soyhan; Vatican museum sign © istockphoto.com/Nikada; Puddle on St Peter's Square © istockphoto.com/spooh; Statue of St Peter in Vatican © istockphoto.com/DHuss; St Paul © istockphoto.com/Matthew71.

6  5  4  3  2  1          Printed in 121          14  15  16  17  18  19

MIX
Paper from
responsible sources

FSC
www.fsc.org     FSC® C004071

# THE LAST THIRTEEN

## BOOK TWO

# JAMES PHELAN

**Scholastic Canada Ltd.**
Toronto  New York  London  Auckland  Sydney
Mexico City  New Delhi  Hong Kong  Buenos Aires

# PREVIOUSLY

Sam has a vivid nightmare. A frightening masked figure confronts him, setting everything alight, and Sam wakes up in a cold sweat.

❁

Armed soldiers snatch Sam from his school classroom. On the way to an unknown location, their helicopter is attacked. Sam and two other prisoners—Alex and Eva—survive the crash.

❁

Sam is alarmed when a woman he saw in his nightmare shows up. She takes them to safety at a mountaintop hideaway in the Swiss Alps. There, at the Academy, the headmaster explains that they are true Dreamers and that Sam is part of a prophecy foretelling of the last 13 Dreamers racing against evil to save the world.

❁

Sam's nightmare comes true in New York when he battles to capture the Star of Egypt and comes face to face with the monster from his nightmare, Solaris. Sam fights for his life but Solaris overwhelms him, choking him . . .

## SAM

"This is where you die, Sam . . ."

The veins bulged in Sam's head as he grit his teeth in pain.

*I am not ready to die.*

Sam pounded at the arm wrapped tight around his neck but his enemy's grip was too strong. He desperately tried to break free as the sound of the oncoming train grew louder.

*Use your opponent's force against them . . . that's it!*

Sam suddenly stopped struggling and leaned forward to take the weight of Solaris on his back. He staggered quickly toward the train tracks. With his last bit of strength, Sam heaved him over, finally breaking free of the stranglehold and reeling back from the platform edge. Solaris landed on the tracks with a loud thud and lay motionless.

Sam crashed to his knees, gasping, hungry for air. Turning, he stumbled to the bench seat, reached out to it and picked up the Star of Egypt. By the dim light of the emergency lighting system in the subway station, he saw his reflection in the smooth crystal surface and wiped away blood from a cut on his lip.

*Finally* . . . Sam looked back in the direction of the tracks. No movement. *It's over.*

He began to walk away—then stopped cold. He felt a presence behind him.

Sam turned in time to see Solaris climb up onto the platform. *No! It can't be.*

"Going somewhere, boy?"

Sam edged back a step. *I don't think I have another fight like that left in me.*

He brought up his hands, forcing himself into a defensive stance as Solaris approached menacingly. *I can do this. I must do this.*

The train thundered past at high speed, the carriage lights flashing across Sam's face, throwing Solaris into shadow.

Sam braced in a side stance, ready for the onslaught as the dark figure started to run toward him.

*PFFT! PFFT!*

Sam ducked, his hands over his head.

Silence.

Sam looked up and saw Solaris crumple to the ground. Then there was no movement, no sound but Solaris' rasping breaths through the mask.

Sam could see two darts protruding from the exposed and suddenly very human-looking neck, the chest moving up and down slowly. Sam spun around to find the shooter but could see no one. He reached down for the mask. *I have to know . . .*

As Sam's fingers curled around the bottom of the mask, he steadied himself, preparing for . . . who knew what? No one had ever seen this creature before.

He pulled hard and fell back as he recognized the face.

*The female Enterprise Agent . . . the woman from the alleyway who fired the rocket launcher!*

"She'll be fine."

Sam jumped at the sound of the voice behind him. He looked up and saw . . .

*Shiva?*

He was standing over Sam, dart gun in hand.

"She—" Sam turned back to the unconscious figure. "She, Solaris, was in my dream—she was going to kill us all!"

"No," Shiva said, "that's not Solaris."

"What?" *But the suit, the metallic, scrambled voice . . . that was Solaris, right?*

"That's not the *real* figure from your dream. She's an impostor." Shiva glanced around, alert. *Does he think the real Solaris might be close by?*

"But . . ." Sam gazed at the mask in his hands. It seemed about right, but now he saw it this close, he realized that it wasn't exactly as he had seen it in his dream. This mask was smaller, especially the respirator section covering the mouth. This was someone trying to dress like Solaris, to appear like him . . . it. "But how did she know what he looked like?"

"The Enterprise must have hacked into your dream recording at the Academy," Shiva said. "This woman, Stella, is in charge of the field Agents, the ones who go out on operations. She's wearing a second-generation Stealth Suit, adapted to mimic Solaris. And that mask—well, it's not standard issue. Looks like it's from the toy shop."

"A toy shop?"

"*The* toy shop—our research and development lab, they make all our equipment."

"Why didn't you warn us about her?" Sam asked.

"Because . . ." he looked down at his feet, "I had no idea. This doesn't make any sense. Either no one at the Enterprise knows, or I'm not cleared for that information . . ."

"No one at the Enterprise knows?"

"I don't think she's here representing the Enterprise. Not like this, shooting at you in the alleyway. Maybe she's gone rogue."

"She shot down our jet . . ." Sam said. His voice faltered. The sprinklers in the museum above continued to spray a steady stream of water that cascaded down through the gaping hole in the ceiling of the subway station, flooding onto the tiled floor around them.

"Well, she must have gone out on her own, with help, I guess. But this is not the work of the Enterprise, they . . . I . . . we would never do something like shoot down an aircraft. Never. We're not murderers."

"But Stella *is* Enterprise—and *you're* Enterprise!" Sam

said, standing up and facing Shiva. "And you tricked us at the café!"

"The police will be coming. Sam, you should go." Shiva backed off, looking toward the ceiling.

"You gave us a fake Star of Egypt!" Sam yelled, anger burning through him. "You're a part of this!"

"We're all a part of this, Sam. I gave you that in order to buy time and get the real crystal to you."

"Why?" Sam demanded.

"I figured someone was watching me." Shiva stared down at Stella, whose Stealth Suit had changed back into a default charcoal-coloured suit now that her mind was no longer controlling its appearance. "And now I know why."

Sam shook his head, disbelieving. "You set off that smoke grenade."

"And it saved us all. If Stella knew that I'd met with you and Lora, I'd be done for . . ." The shouts of firefighters rang out above them. "You need to go, Sam. Take the Star and get out of here. Go, Sam—now!"

"Where do I go?"

"Wherever your dreams take you," Shiva said.

"But . . ." Sam stammered, confused. "The dream is finished—it's over. It didn't even happen completely the way I dreamed it, the things we changed made it different. But that's all I had to go by, how should I know what to do next?"

"There will be more dreams, Sam. You're the first of the

last 13. There's a long way to go. In any case, you've got what you came for."

Sam looked at the crystal in his hand.

"You got what you dreamed, that's all that matters here. And remember," Shiva said, "be wary of who you trust. A secret's worth is calculated by those from whom it must be kept."

Sam nodded.

Shiva sighed, looking at the destruction all around them. "Time for you to go before there are too many difficult questions and more people looking for you and what you have," he gestured toward the Star. "And I'll make sure Lora is OK, don't worry. Good luck, Sam."

Sam ran through the subway tunnel, the Star of Egypt heavy in his hand and Shiva's words burning in his ears . . . *be wary of who you trust . . .*

He nearly tripped on the tracks but kept sprinting as fast as he could. A million questions spun through his mind. *Where do I go now? Who can I trust? Where is everyone else? How do I find out what to do with the Star of Egypt?*

There was light ahead, a dull glow. *Is that another subway station?* Then he heard the rattling hum and vibrations of an oncoming train.

"Oh, boy . . ."

Sam couldn't turn back now, he'd never make it. He ran on, searching the walls, the ceiling, scanning everywhere until he saw the rungs of a steel ladder up ahead, leading up a wall and to a manhole above.

The train was getting closer. The ladder seemed impossibly far away. *I'm not going to make it!* Sam pushed himself harder and ran for his life. He clutched the crystal, desperate to keep it safe. *Maybe it would have been smarter to try my luck with the firefighters*. But Sam knew he couldn't have risked it.

The screeching noise of the train was getting louder, and the rungs were still metres away. He ran with everything he had, his aching legs burning with the effort. Hot wind whooshed toward him, and Sam knew he was out of time.

He squeezed into the ladder recess with only a millisecond to spare before the train flashed past. He clung tightly to a steel rung, holding his breath, as the wind of the train blasting through the tunnel threatened to suck him out and into the path of the rattling carriages.

Finally, the train passed and the sound faded away.

Sam went limp, for a moment giving in to his exhausted body and mind. His heart rate slowed as he put the crystal into his pocket. He gripped the ladder and made the climb up slowly, his arms and legs heavy, weak. At the top, he pushed with his back against the manhole cover, again and again, straining with all he had left. Eventually it budged and he prised it up enough to squeeze through, slipping out into the middle of a wet street, rain pounding down.

He stood across the street from the museum. Fire-engines, police cars and ambulances had converged and firefighters, cops and paramedics spilled out over the museum steps. Hundreds of black-tie patrons were huddling together, shocked, wet and cold.

"Need a lift?"

Sam froze. He knew that voice.

"Hey, Xavier," Sam said, as he turned toward his classmate.

"You OK?" Xavier asked.

"Yeah," Sam said, dusting himself off. "Just—just tired, I guess. That was intense."

"Yeah, you can say that again."

Sam looked across the road and watched as Lora was stretchered out. Eva was beside her, holding her hand while the paramedics loaded Lora into the back of an ambulance. *At least I know Eva's safe. I should go over there.* But at that moment, the ambulance drove off, lights flashing as it went past. He watched it disappear in the mess of lights in the night.

Xavier said, "You need a ride someplace?"

Sam ignored him, though not on purpose. He was busy wondering where Tobias and Alex had ended up. *Hopefully they're back at the safe house, making plans to get Lora and Eva back to the Academy. I'll think about that later.* Sam forced himself back into the present.

He turned to Xavier and asked, "Where are you headed?"

"Where do *you* need to go?" Xavier replied, holding open the door of the waiting limo.

Sam smiled, a little confused, but considering all that was going on around them, he wanted to get off the street and out of sight. He got into the back seat of the car.

"Where's your dad?" Sam asked.

"He's got a couple of bruises and a concussion. He'll be fine. He and the mayor went in an ambulance together," Xavier said, shutting the door behind them and rapping his knuckles on the dark glass partition to signal to the driver. "My father will be out of it for a bit, which suits me just fine. He's been driving me crazy lately, what with this exhibition and all—and you should have seen him freak out when I told him how you'd been taken out from school."

"That seems like it happened ages ago . . ." Sam settled into the comfy leather seat. His aching bones were grateful to rest.

"Are you really on some secret-agent mission?" Xavier asked, a glint in his eye. He got a couple of bottles of lemonade out from a minibar and passed one to Sam.

"Thanks. And yeah, something like that," Sam replied, gulping it down.

The limo drove through the police lines and onto the street, heading away from the museum. A series of recent memories flashed through Sam's mind.

*For every action there is an equal and opposite reaction . . .*

*It could reveal everything we need to know to win the battle.*

*Blame yourself—you brought us here.*

*Just trust that the right thing will happen.*

"Well, I want to help you out any way I can," Xavier said. "Wherever you need to go, just say the word, I'll get you there."

"And why would you want to do that?" Sam asked, instantly suspicious.

"Would you believe," Xavier said slowly, "that I dreamed it?"

"Dreamed it?" Sam looked at him, shocked. *Could it be?*

"Last night," Xavier chuckled to himself. "Crazy, eh? I dreamed that I saw my dad getting put into an ambulance and that you'd ride in this limo with me. Then you and I were in his jet, flying east."

Sam was lost for words. Xavier waited in silence. Sam's fingers touched the smooth surface of the Star of Egypt nestled in his pocket and suddenly he knew where he had to go. The Star of *Egypt*, the *Egyptian* Dream Stele. Answers needed to be found and the source of this knowledge, of these artifacts, seemed too much of a coincidence to ignore.

*Shiva was right—there was a clue in the Star. Time to trust my instincts.*

Sam cleared his throat and said as calmly as he could, "Say, your private jet . . . it's a big one, right?"

"Yeah, it can go anywhere, and it's fast . . ."

"Nice."

Xavier grinned. "Sounds like you know where we're going?"

Sam nodded, pulling out the Star and opening his hand to reveal the glittering crystal sphere. "You ever been to Egypt?"

## SAM'S NIGHTMARE

**"W**e have to jump," I say. I look down from the balcony to the terrace below. There are people everywhere, music is blaring and underneath us is a large cake lit up with candles. "We can make it, trust me."

"Are you joking?" the girl gasps, shaking her head, a mass of dark brown curls tumbling around her pretty face. "You must be out of your mind!"

"Look, I know it's a lot to take in but you have to believe me." I tilt my head to listen to a commotion outside.

"Because my life depends on it, is that what you said?" Her grey, almond-shaped eyes narrow as she stands with her hands on her hips. Although petite, she somehow fills the space with her presence.

"Yes, and we have to leave right—"

*SMASH!* Someone has slammed against the door.

"—now!"

Two massive guys burst into the room.

"What is it?" she yells at them.

"Security breach," the biggest guy says. "We have to get you to a safe—"

Before he can finish, he and his comrade slump forward, several small darts sticking in their backs. I grab the girl and pull her onto the railing next to me.

*WHACK!*

A dart hits the doorframe behind my head, its barbed end sticking into the timber.

*That was close!*

I see a group of Enterprise Agents storming the room, dressed like ninjas, their intention clear.

"What the−?" the girl is stunned.

Without hesitation, I drop down onto a flower bed on the terrace below, taking her with me, and roll onto my side.

*Argh! I've hurt my ankle.*

"Hurry!" I say, dragging the girl to her feet and running as best I can. We hide under the cover of the terrace as the Enterprise Agents send more darts fizzing through the air around us. "We need to get out of here, fast!"

She turns to me and yells, "Follow me!"

Time jumps and I see my fingernails dig into the dashboard of a sports car. The girl weaves through traffic like a Hollywood stunt driver, in and out of the lanes of oncoming cars as horns blaze all around us.

"Are they still back there?" she says.

I feel sick as I twist in the seat to look for . . .

"Yes!" I answer, not believing my own ears as I say to her, "Faster! Go faster!"

Another time jump and we run from the car and along a dark corridor. The girl speaks to uniformed guards and we're let through a steel gate and descend a stone staircase. More guards and a few doors later . . .

"Wow!"

"*Ma dai!*" she says.

"Huh?"

"Come on!" she says, pulling me through a dark maze, the walls towering high above us.

We skid to a stop and contemplate the way ahead. In the dim light, I make out more details of the labyrinth. The walls are in fact shelves, at least twice as tall as me, holding stacks and stacks of books.

"This way," she says, pulling me by the hand as we run through a canyon of bound volumes.

"Shh!" I say as we turn a corner and I pull her to a stop. I feel my heart beating fast and try to calm it as I whisper, "Someone's talking, nearby . . . listen."

Further away, there is the frantic pattering of footfalls. Our pursuers are after us—it sounds like they've broken into two groups. The talking stops.

A man appears before us. "Argh!" I reel back, startled by the luminous whites of his oversized eyes. He has the look of someone who's been in the dark with books for a *long* time.

I run deeper into the darkness but I've lost her—I can't even call out her name. I look all around me and it's completely dark.

I realize I'm in a tunnel. It's cold and as I run, dread creeps over me like a heavy blanket. I feel dust coat my face, now it's in my mouth and I cough loudly.

I see two separate tunnels ahead—I aim for the right one, desperate to reach it. But I'm not running anymore, I'm swimming. *I'm in water?*

"It's too late, Sam. You can't escape."

That metallic voice—Solaris. Evil radiates from him.

I've made the tunnel, but I have no weapons, it's just me and him. And the fire that I dread. He begins to laugh as I flinch from his outstretched arms.

I hear screams above and all around me. *Where is she?* I need to save her, but it is too dark, and rocks are raining down on me like an avalanche. I have to escape, I cannot fail. The tunnel is closing in around me. I am trapped. *It's the roof, the roof is coming down on me!*

"Help me!" I scream out, gasping for air. "What can I do?" My voice echoes into the sudden silence all around me. "Where are you?"

The rocks are crushing me, and there's a searing white light and an explosion of sound and heat. And everything is—

Lost.

## SAM

**S**am woke up gasping for breath and coughing. He looked up into the sky above him. It was full of stars and as he lifted his head, he could make out a string of city lights far below him that looked like a mirror image of the sky stretched out against the wider darkness. His right hand held what felt like a huge glass marble . . . *it's the Star of Egypt.* Its polished surface shimmered faintly in the dim light.

He turned his head slowly and saw a dark figure snoring gently next to him. Xavier. *Where am I?* he wondered hazily. But curiosity about the hard, gritty surface beneath him wasn't enough to keep him awake as sleep overtook him once again. *Just a few minutes more.*

When Sam woke again, gentle sunlight bathed his face and he was warm. He rolled over, eyes still closed for a moment. The screeching of a train and the memory of gasping for air washed over him. New York, and the Solaris that wasn't Solaris. But there was something else—a vivid dream, but he couldn't quite recall it. A dream of running from . . . *someone* . . . and he'd been buried underneath something, and then . . . *what?* He remembered waking, looking up at stars. Now the sun was blinding through his eyelids. *Where am I?*

His eyes flew open with shocking clarity. He was not in his bed. He was not in *any* bed. He was lying on hard, dusty stones.

Sam sat up. His arm was asleep and his back ached.

"Oh, man!"

He scrambled to his knees, groggy and exhausted, and as he looked around, the Sphinx came into view. Shocked, Sam looked down at the hundreds of giant stone steps below him. He leaned over to the still-slumbering Xavier and jabbed him. "Xavier, wake up. Wake up!"

"Hmph?" Xavier rolled away from Sam and continued to snore.

Sam shuffled to the edge of the massive slab of weathered limestone. He stood and looked down at the view and there was no mistaking it. He was at a place he'd seen in books and on TV and in movies a thousand times, only never quite from *this* vantage point.

*I'm on top of the Great Pyramid of Giza!*

His throat was dry and his stomach rumbled with hunger. His hands were dirty and dusty and caked in dry blood. His feet ached, and pulling up his pant legs he saw he'd scraped his knees and shins.

*We climbed all the way up here?*

"Xavier!" Sam pushed him harder this time. Xavier began to mumble and stretch.

The events of last night came flooding back. Xavier had given him a ride to Egypt in his private jet. It had seemed like such a cool thing to do at the time, to climb a pyramid. To have an adventure that didn't involve the fate of the world. But the newspaper article the Professor had shown him made him nervous now. Those deadly treasure hunters had caused havoc outside Cairo—near where they were right now. *What if the Pyramid was a target? Are there things buried around here that Solaris or someone else in the race might find useful?* Sam struggled to remember more of the article.

But there was another memory. Something he knew he was meant to remember . . . *I woke up in the night!* He'd woken, on top of the pyramid and seen stars. He'd woken from a dream. *The dream! What happened in the dream?*

Try as he might, his mind was a blank, his memory of the dream nothing more than a shadowy fog. *Seriously, after everything the Professor told me, and Dr. Dark . . . and I can't remember a thing? That fight with Solaris must have really scrambled my brain. Some food might help . . .*

Sam looked down the side of the pyramid and saw tourists already milling around down there, as small as ants. By the time he and Xavier would get even halfway down, there'd probably be thousands of them.

But there, on the stone step just below them, something glinted in the sun.

*The Star of Egypt.*

Sam went to the edge, lowered himself down to the next step and landed in a heap. *Great, just a couple hundred more of these to go to get all the way down.*

He reached for the dark sapphire sphere and stopped—it was broken, cracked in half. The golden star shape within was what had caught the glint of the sun. With the nausea of failure rising in his stomach, Sam wondered how he could take such news back to the Academy. *Sorry, Professor, I managed to beat Solaris to the Star of Egypt, I managed to travel to the other side of the world with it. Then, I had an accident . . . oops.*

Sam picked up the two pieces and did a double take, staring at them in wonder.

"What the . . . ?"

## EVA

Eva stood in the middle of Times Square, in the bustle of the hot summer night. Crazy sights and sounds surrounded her—people brushing past, snapping photos and laughing, but it was all just background noise. The news of the jet explosion still echoed in her ears, the shock still fresh, although she'd been told hours ago. Even late at night, there were thousands of people here, but she felt completely alone. Just like that, quick as you could click your fingers, the jet had crashed down into a city street and changed everything.

And Sam? *Where is he?* Eva was anxious. Sam hadn't been seen since he fell into the tunnels beneath the museum.

Lora appeared next to her. "Our pick-up is within the hour."

Eva nodded. She studied Lora, who never stopped watching the people around them, always alert. Lora had explained this was a good place to hide because of the crowds.

"Are you OK?" Eva asked.

"I'm fine," Lora said, fiddling nervously with the bandage around her arm.

"I mean, you were unconscious. Don't you think you should—"

"I'm not going to wait around in some hospital," Lora said, "when Sam, Tobias and Alex are out there somewhere."

Eva nodded, appreciating Lora's sentiment. *She's not that much older than me, but she seems so protective—like an older sister.* Lora made eye contact with her. There were tears streaking silently down her face. Sebastian had been her boyfriend, after all. Eva had known him—and the rest of them—for only three days. *Three days . . .* in such a short time she'd been told that she was a true Dreamer, and that a race was on to find thirteen special Dreamers who could not only dream things that were true but were somehow part of an ancient prophecy to save—

"We have to move!" Lora said. Before Eva could blink, she was dragged across the street and led down to a subway station, Lora pushing hard through the masses, leaving protesters in their wake.

"Quick!" she said, vaulting the turnstiles and pulling Eva through the closing doors of the subway carriage. Lora watched the platform until it was left far behind them.

"What was it?" Eva asked as the train rattled along the tunnel. It took a moment for Lora to answer. Eva could tell that Lora was at once full of rage and sadness.

"Enterprise Agents," Lora replied. "They're still tracking us. We have to ditch them before we get our lift back to the Academy."

Eva and Lora got out at Grand Central Terminal and walked through another throng of people, exiting against the flow of the late-night crowd leaving the city after dinners and shows.

Lora pulled out her phone while she hailed a taxi.

"Do you think they're gone?" Eva asked.

"No, they're still out there," Lora said. She told the driver to take them to the airport.

"Are we safe?"

"We're never completely safe, Eva. Not from the Enterprise and certainly not from Solaris. You have to remember that, OK?" Her call connected and she began to speak into the phone. It was the Professor. "She's with me—have you heard from Tobias?" There was a long pause as Lora listened. Eva looked out the window as they crossed a bridge over the East River.

Lora continued to talk, "Clearly with the prophecy coming true, our agreement with the Enterprise can no longer be relied on to . . . yes, Professor, I agree. And we've no other information so far about the woman? . . . I don't think it was Solaris—taking down an aircraft like that.

It doesn't make sense. Seb wasn't one of the last 13, why would he be a target? No, I think it was entirely that Agent's idea. Maybe she was trying to prove something with that ruthless display, but to who? . . . I don't know what to say, I can't believe he's gone." Lora's voice cracked. She turned away as Eva reached over to take her hand. Lora pulled herself together and switched on the speaker function and held the phone between them. "Professor, Eva is here."

"Eva? Are you alright, my dear?" the Professor said.

"I'm OK," Eva said.

"It's been a terrible night," he said, "but we'll get you home to us soon, stay strong. I'm just happy that Tobias had the foresight to send you on to the museum to meet Lora and Sam. We're fortunate that your escort turned out to be on our side."

"But I'm so worried about Sam and Alex, and the others who are missing," Eva said. "Why did some of the Guardians turn on us?"

"We know those Guardians were an elite group from Egypt—Lora spotted their scarab insignia at the museum. Now the race has begun, the Council think they might have another agenda, that they believe the world is best protected by preventing the prophecy from being fulfilled. That would explain why they destroyed the Dream Stele."

"And the helicopter?" Eva gasped. "Could it have been them that tried to kill us by shooting down the helicopter?"

"I think that's a distinct possibility. But it's going to be

OK," Lora said, putting her arm around Eva's shoulders. "We've got Guardians, ones we can trust, looking after us now. We can do this Eva, all of us. We'll learn from this. We're going to fight them with everything we have."

*But Sam's the key to all of this and we don't even know where he is or if he's safe. What if we can't do it without him?*

Eva swallowed and summoned the courage to ask, "How do we have any hope of beating Solaris? I mean, if Sam is . . . if he's gone, what chance do we have?"

"Eva, we have no reason to believe that Sam isn't still alive and well," Lora said. "He's one of the last 13, it's his destiny to see this through, and all the competing parties know that. No Sam, no race."

"I wouldn't be surprised," the Professor said over the phone, a smile in his voice, "if right now, Sam was ploughing on with the race with the Star of Egypt in his back pocket, saving the world all on his own."

## SAM

**S**am held the Star of Egypt gingerly in his hands. He stared at the two halves, but his dread at breaking it had evaporated. Before him, inside this seemingly solid glass ball, was an object. Now it was clear that the sapphire's sparkle was more than just colours changing in the light. Inside there was an *actual gold object*. It sat there, still nestled within the gem. Sam picked at an edge of the gold, inspecting it closely, then held it up to the sun. It looked like a small handle with a star-shaped head. With some shaking, tapping and prying, the golden star pulled free.

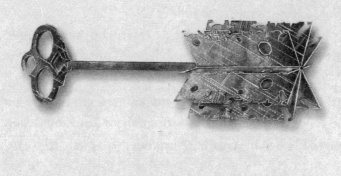

*A key?*

It was unlike any key he'd ever seen before.

Xavier peered over his shoulder. "Interesting . . . you've excavated the Star of Egypt, I see."

There was a noise from down below, a shout, as though from a bullhorn—they'd been spotted. They looked at each other and grimaced.

*Time to go.*

Sam took off the leather strap that hung around his neck, opened the clasp and slipped on the key. It dangled down next to the dream catcher that Tobias had given to him. He slipped it back over his head, under his shirt and pocketed the two half-spheres of the Star of Egypt.

"Let's get moving."

"Ancient . . . Egyptians . . . hmph!" Sam said, as he and Xavier crawled and tumbled their way down the Great Pyramid's block-like steps. "Why'd . . . they . . . have to build . . . this thing . . . so tall?"

"It didn't . . . seem . . . so big . . . last night," Xavier puffed next to him.

"You know, I once read a book by a guy who climbed Everest. He said getting up a mountain was only half the job and it's often the getting *down* that's more dangerous." Sam paused to catch his breath. "Turns out that's pretty true, eh?"

"Ouch!" Xavier grimaced as they both slid down another ledge, scraping their arms painfully.

They collapsed onto the edge of a stone step for a breather. The broken sphere halves weighed heavily in Sam's pockets. It might well be worthless now, but he couldn't leave it behind, especially since he knew the cost of getting it. The Professor's son, Sebastian, was on the jet that was shot out of the sky and he'd seen Lora loaded into an ambulance outside the Museum of Natural History.

Sam felt especially guilty about that now, nauseous even. He'd left her and Eva, climbed into Xavier's limo and gotten out of town in a hurry.

His thoughts added urgency to the task ahead—finding the information he needed and getting back to the Academy so he could continue in the race against Solaris.

Looking down, Sam could see they were still practically at the top of the pyramid.

"There's gotta be an easier way . . ."

There wasn't.

They navigated the gigantic time-worn stone steps as best they could but the steps were uneven at the edges, making the going hard.

"Argh!" Xavier tumbled off a step and the momentum took him rolling down two more steps before he fell into a heap and got to his hands and knees. He sat himself down at the edge, his feet dangling over the next block. Looking back up at Sam's concerned face, Xavier made an "OK" sign with his fingers. But it was what Sam saw below that worried him.

A group of tourists had come together and were pointing up at them. Two security guards stood down there too—arms firmly crossed over their uniforms, badges and weapons gleaming in the scorching sun.

*Great. When we do make it down, we're going to have some serious explaining to do.*

## ALEX

Alex came to in a world of lights and sounds, all piercing his skull. He tried to open his eyes but they resisted, aching with the effort. *Wake up, Alex, wake up!* His eyes opened but it didn't really help. *Where am I?*

He sucked in deep, ragged breaths as he lay prone on the hard ground, then shivered. The last thing he remembered was looking up from an empty backstreet at the Academy aircraft just half a block away from him as he'd made his way to the café to meet Sam and Lora. Alex had seen Sebastian pull the jet away and then turn into a sharp banking manoeuvre as—

As a missile streaked through the air, followed by an explosion, the super-hot heat of it . . . *then what?*

Air rushing, pushing on him so he couldn't breathe, and then he'd blacked out. *Was I blown clear by the force of the explosion? I was practically underneath, so close, and survived. Could Sebastian be OK?*

*No. No way anyone made it out of that wreck alive.*

*What about me? Is this a dream or am I dead?*

He focused on the sounds around him . . . *sirens, bells?* He struggled to sit up and then stand. There was muddy water up to his ankles, coating him all over. *How much has it rained? No wonder I was cold.*

He tried to call out for help, but with the ringing in his ears he couldn't tell if he was making a sound or not. His throat was dry and sore. His clothes were singed and torn in places. Heavy rain fell upon his face.

He turned to look around—

*KLANG!*

He bumped straight into something hard.

Next to him on the road, just a few centimetres from where he stood, was a car, thrown over on its side from the explosion.

He reached out a muddy hand and grabbed hold of the car to steady himself. It was a new VW Beetle, practically a convertible now.

"So much for indestructible German engineering . . ."

All around him on the street he could see police and fire department cordons around the block. Cars were ablaze and the entire scene was littered with debris. A war zone. The aircraft wreckage was smouldering, firefighters were dousing it with white foam.

*No way anyone survived that . . .*

In the side mirror of the wrecked car he saw himself— covered with a layer of dirt and mud, just the whites of his eyes showing . . . in that moment, his world seemed to spin and went dark.

## SAM

"You have no passport, no ID . . . nothing but this," the security guard said, inspecting Sam's phone and throwing it to his colleague, "which doesn't seem to work. But your friend is more lucky, I think." Xavier's leather wallet, designer sunglasses and expensive phone lay on the rickety metal table between them. An ineffectual ceiling fan whined above them, moving the oppressive air slowly around the windowless security office.

Sam and Xavier were wisely silent. The guard sitting opposite them had a badge pinned on his grey shirt that read "Hasani." He was the hairiest man Sam had ever seen. The one standing closer to them—"Nizam" his badge declared—was tall and mean-looking, with the most disgusting bad breath Sam had ever encountered.

"You were found," Nizam said, "at the base of our Great Pyramid, where you'd fallen down, having broken the law by climbing upon our sacred structure."

Sam replied, "We were just trying to get off your—your sacred structure."

The guard oozed anger from every pungent pore.

*All that effort to get down,* Sam thought, *to fall into a heap amid a flurry of tourists snapping pictures as we were hauled away by security.* He looked over at Xavier. They both looked as though they were made of sand, covered from head to toe in dust.

*The Sandmen versus the Hairy Beast and Toilet Breath.*

The two guards continued to take turns to quiz them.

"When did you climb up?"

Sam shrugged. "Last night, I guess."

"What's your business here?"

"We have no business," Sam said, "we're fifteen years old. What business would we have?"

Xavier muttered, "Business like fart breath here?"

Sam chuckled.

"Tell us again!" Nizam said, jamming his face into Sam's. "The truth this time!"

*Ew! Please don't talk to me that close.*

Hasani said, "How did you get into Egypt?"

"As we said," Sam replied, his eyes watering, "we *can't remember* how we got here." *Don't make it any worse for Xavier.* Mentioning a private jet seemed like a bad idea, especially when Sam recalled how Xavier had bribed the customs people to let them in without any hassle.

Xavier sat calmly next to him, smiling. Unfortunately, his suave charm was lost on the Egyptian guards.

Hasani slammed his palm down onto the table. "Then

you will stay here until you remember!"

All Sam could think about was that this situation could lead the Enterprise Agents straight to him. *They're probably closing in on me right now. Then what? What will they do with me? What will they do with Xavier? I shouldn't have dragged him into this. He was so willing to help me because of his dream. Even without really knowing what I was up to.*

"And this," Nizam said, looking at the broken Star of Egypt on the table, "looks old."

"And expensive," Hasani added. "Did you *steal* this?"

"Did you steal it and then break it?" Nizam asked.

"That could be a costly mistake," Hasani menaced.

Sam shook his head in exasperation. Thankfully they'd not noticed the leather strap around his neck, the key still safely tucked inside his shirt. Not that anyone could tell where his skin finished and his clothes began for all the dust and grime.

Xavier cut into his thoughts, "Can we please call our embassy if we're going to continue to be held like this? My father is a powerful man—"

"Powerful, you say?" Nizam interrupted.

"And rich," Xavier said. "He can reward you."

"We look like we need rewards?" The veiled threat was somehow also an invitation.

*No, but you could do with a shower and some mouthwash.*

Xavier said, "And I think he's going to have a lot to say about this kind of heavy-handed treatment of what was merely a schoolboy prank. We were bored. The pyramid was there. We climbed it."

The guards turned their backs on the boys for a brief, animated discussion.

"I have good news for you," Nizam said as he turned back to face them. "I have convinced my friend that you are too much trouble to worry about on a hot, busy day like today. We have many, many tourists from all over the world who deserve our attention more than you."

"All that it takes for us to forget this happened is a little compensation for our time," Hasani said evenly, staring intently at Xavier.

"Are you suggesting—" Sam's outrage overtaking his common sense.

"Sam, Sam," Xavier cautioned. "Gentlemen, it was a pleasure to have this discussion with you on the need for sensitivity and respect for cultural heritage. Please take this," Xavier pulled out a bundle of notes from his wallet and held them out, "as a small donation to the upkeep of this historic site."

Nizam snatched the money in a heartbeat, smirking as he stuffed the notes into his shirt pocket.

"But listen to me, schoolboys," Hasani said, "if we catch you anywhere near the pyramids again, there will be no more good news, or donations. Only a long wait in a very small cell. Understand?" He flung open the office door and motioned them out.

"Go now," Nizam ordered.

Sam hastily grabbed the Star and his phone as they were led to the front door and then unceremoniously shoved outside.

Blinking in the blinding light, Sam's eyes watered again. "Xavier, you OK?"

"Never better," he grinned as he slipped on his sunglasses. "You?" he asked.

"Yeah." Sam looked at his hands, red raw from the pyramid climb.

"Come on, let's get cleaned up," Xavier said. "We didn't really check out the hotel much last night when we arrived. I think there's a pool, maybe we could squeeze in a swim." He smiled lazily.

Sam marvelled at his composure.

*Nothing seems to faze him.*

The office doorway gave out onto a side street full of parked tourist buses and hawkers selling plastic pyramid souvenirs. As Sam looked for a taxi, there was a toot of horns and a flurry of people across the street to their right. When Sam turned around, he thought for a moment he saw a flash of a familiar grey suit and black tie. An Enterprise Agent? *Surely not. Not already.*

"Maybe . . . we shouldn't go back to our hotel," he said.

"You getting popular again?" Xavier said, flagging down a taxi. "Plan B—my father has an old friend in Cairo, he'll help us."

"You're sure this is the right address?" Sam asked.

The dwelling before them was a tiny stone house, sandwiched between dilapidated concrete apartment blocks.

"Sure as I'm a Dark," Xavier said, then pointed. "See here?"

A brass plaque next to the door read *Dr. Ahmed Kader,* and there was a letter hanging out of the mailbox from Dark Corp, Xavier's family business. Xavier pressed the bell.

There was no sound.

They waited.

Xavier pressed again. Sam tried knocking.

"Maybe there's—"

An unlocking noise came from behind the door and cut Sam off, then it opened.

A short, rotund man stood before them. He was only half as high as the doorway but nearly as wide. "Xavier! This is a wonderful surprise!" Dr. Kader said, his face breaking into a big friendly smile underneath a bushy moustache. "Welcome my boy, come in, come in!"

Sam followed Xavier inside.

The hallway was long and dark, leading to a small courtyard. They sat at a table under a large gnarled fig tree while Dr. Kader put a kettle on the boil.

"Dr. Kader—"

"Ahmed, my dear Xavier, Ahmed. You don't need to call your godfather anything more than that. Unless he deserves less, of course!" Dr. Kader chuckled as he gathered together a tea jug, bunches of mint and a big jar of honey.

"Ahmed," Xavier said, "this is my school friend, Sam."

"Sam, good to meet you," he said, his rough hand shaking Sam's, his eyes searching. "I must say, Sam, you look familiar . . ."

"You may have seen me on TV this morning. Xavier and I made the local news, I think." Sam wasn't certain he'd seen TV cameras when they'd gotten off the pyramid, but it would explain how the Enterprise might have found them . . .

Xavier laughed and Ahmed shook his head. "No, no televisions in this house," he said. "Evil business they are."

Sam shrugged.

"Sounds like you boys have been busy, though. Tea?"

"Thanks," Sam said, and watched as Ahmed poured tea into three ornate glasses. He sat and faced them, the aged wooden bench beneath him creaking.

"Please have some kahk—they're a traditional Egyptian delicacy, and I know Xavier enjoys them," Ahmed said with a smile as he passed over a plate of delicious-looking sugar-coated cookies. "So, to what do I owe the honour of your visit? Has your father finally seen sense and sent you here for some hands-on study out in the field?"

"Not yet," Xavier said, taking his tea and raising it. "To your health, dear Ahmed."

"Thank you, I will take that toast and second it," he said, laughing as the three of them clinked glasses.

"We're here because . . ." Xavier trailed off, looking to Sam to explain.

"I had to come here, to Egypt," Sam said. "I need to find out more about this artifact."

He placed the two halves of the Star of Egypt onto the table.

Ahmed put on the glasses hanging loose on a chain around his beefy neck and studied the two hemispheres carefully but quickly.

"Ah yes . . . well, it is old but not ancient," Ahmed chuckled. "And certainly not Egyptian."

Xavier looked as shocked as Sam felt.

"But," Xavier protested, "this was part of my father's new exhibit."

"Yes, I know of it," Ahmed said. "I warned your father that the collection was contaminated."

"Contaminated?"

"It was not all of the same era. Some Egyptian antiquities, no doubt, but some other more recent relics among them, including this. This is a good likeness of the ancient

Egyptian original, but it is definitely from the Renaissance."

"The Renaissance?" Xavier said.

"Early 16th century, I'd say."

"How do you know?"

"Because it's the work of a genius," Ahmed said, holding one half-sphere. "It was designed as two parts, as a vessel."

"Who designed it?" Sam asked, avoiding Xavier's curious gaze for the moment, shifting a little in his seat and feeling the weight of the golden key around his neck, hidden under his shirt.

"The man who put his maker's mark upon it," Ahmed said, pointing to a microscopic scrawl inside—so tiny it was illegible to the naked eye.

"Wow, those must be powerful glasses!" Xavier laughed.

Dr. Kader chuckled again. "Only because I already know what it says."

"Can you tell us more?" Sam said. "Do you know who made the sphere?"

"The sphere *and* what it contained," he nodded, grunting as he stood, putting a hand to his lower back. He opened a door that revealed steep stairs leading deep under his house. "I will show you."

"No way!" Sam said. "How can that be?"

But there was no mistaking it. A screen in a surprisingly

high-tech, yet television-free, lab beneath the house showed the hi-res magnification of two signatures, one laid over the other in a perfect match. One was from a well-known painting, the other from the engraving inside the sphere.

*Di Leonardo de Sina*

"Leonardo Da Vinci?"

Ahmed nodded wisely. "As I said, the man was a genius."

"Why'd he make this?" Xavier asked.

"Sam?" Ahmed said, looking expectantly at Sam as though he had the answer.

Sam shrugged.

Ahmed prodded, "Do you have the key?"

"Umm, yes, actually." Sam was startled into revealing the truth before he could decide how much he could trust this man. "How did you know about it, Dr. Kader?"

"Please, call me Ahmed," he replied. "Let's just say, I've been aware of this object, and what it contains, for some time."

Sam hesitated and looked to Xavier who frowned and nodded. *Well, if he's Xavier's godfather . . .* "Alright then, here," Sam said, taking the key off the strap and handing it over.

Ahmed put the golden key under a microscope, zooming in and showing the object from all angles and in incredible detail upon a big screen.

"Is that . . ." Sam waited for the image to sharpen, "writing?"

"Yes . . ."

"What language?"

"It looks like hieroglyphs," Ahmed said.

"*Da Vinci* wrote in ancient Egyptian?" Xavier asked.

"Can you read it?" Sam asked. "Decipher it?"

"I'm not sure," Ahmed replied, inspecting the neat crawl of pictographs up close. "They're not quite like any hieroglyphs I've seen before . . ."

"So, where does that leave us?"

A ringing interrupted them—Xavier's phone. He took the call, muttered into the receiver for a moment, then faced Sam and Ahmed.

"That was my father," Xavier said.

"Is he OK?" Sam asked.

"He's fine—he's not very happy with me, though. Wants to know where his jet's gone. I told him I went to Disneyland with a friend. I don't think he believed me. We'd better get back."

"Sounds like you need to go, Xavier. Here," Ahmed said, handing the key to Sam. "You keep it safe. I think you understand how important it might be." He winked at Sam as he said to Xavier, "Now, let's get you both cleaned up and ready for your journey. Come, this way."

Sam finished his call on his recharged phone and turned to Xavier.

"I need to get back to the Acad—to Switzerland," Sam said. "Eva and Lora, my friends who were with me in New York, are there already."

"Then I'll drop you at Geneva on my way home," Xavier said.

"You're sure?"

"Absolutely," Xavier replied, then tapped his godfather on the shoulder. "We'll leave you to it."

"Yes, yes . . ." Ahmed said, looking up from studying the inscriptions on the images of the golden key and shaking Sam's hand. "I'll see you out. And here, take this, it's my contact details. I will work on things here and see where it leads us." He handed Sam a scrawled note, the writing about as indecipherable as that engraved on the key.

"*Leads us?*" Xavier repeated, puzzled.

"A key is made to fit a lock," Ahmed said with a smile as he took them back out onto the sunny street outside, where he flagged down a taxi.

Sam's eyes flicked up and down the busy street. It felt like he was being watched, but it was near impossible to see anything among the parade of people going about their business in the sprawling city.

"Keep the key safe, Sam," Ahmed said once more.

"Of course," Sam replied, getting into the cab after Xavier.

Ahmed paused, looking across the street and his friendly face turned to a more serious expression.

"Be careful who you trust," he said to Sam, sticking his head into the open car window, "and who you let close to that key."

Sam slept the entire flight, woken only by the touchdown at Geneva. His dreams were full of shadows and mysterious faces. *Should I be remembering all of this? How do I know which dreams are part of the race? I guess I trust my instincts, that's what the Professor would say.*

As they started down the jet's exit stairs, he could see Eva running across the tarmac toward him. Behind her, four big Guardians, distinctive in their dark blue uniforms, stood sentry next to the Academy's helicopter.

"Until next time," Xavier said to Sam.

"Thanks, Xavier," Sam said at the bottom of the stairs. "It's been real. Sure you don't want to come with us?"

"I have to check in with my father—and he'd go ballistic if he knew I took the jet out for a little international jaunt," Xavier replied. "I hope you found what you were looking for in Egypt."

"I think I was meant to meet your godfather," Sam said. *And I'm sure there's a reason you were there too.*

"Well," Xavier said, "I'm here if you need a hand with your National Security stuff . . ."

The two of them laughed.

"You're still not going to tell me what this is really all about?" Xavier asked. "Even after I had that dream about helping you?"

Sam watched Eva rushing over to them.

"You wouldn't believe me," Sam said.

"Try me . . ." Xavier said.

"You'd say I was dreaming," Sam replied with a smile.

"Sam, you won't mention my dream to anyone, will you? I mean—if my dad found out, he'd turn me into a pet project. I really don't need that right now." Xavier looked anxious as Eva got closer.

"Sure," Sam said, knowing just how that might feel. "Your secret's safe with me."

Eva flung herself into Sam and held on tight.

"Hey, you," Sam said, wriggling away from her. "Eva, this is my school friend, Xavier."

"Nice to meet you," Eva said. Sam noticed Xavier's cheeks flushed a little. "OK, we have to hurry back."

"Don't go saving the world without me!" Xavier called after them with a wave as they made for the chopper.

Sam waved back, but with those familiar words ringing in his ears, he couldn't help but think of Alex.

**W**hat about Alex?" Sam asked anxiously as soon as they were on board the helicopter.

Eva sighed and shook her head. "We think he was heading to the café when the plane . . . you know . . . but maybe he didn't get that far."

Silence hung between them for a while, but slowly Eva's questions started to come—who was Xavier, what exactly happened back in New York, why had Sam gone to Egypt, and back to Xavier again.

"His dad's a psychiatrist," Sam said, "and part of some wealthy dynasty. They're big on philanthropy, like funding that collection at the Museum of Natural History."

"Sounds like the shrink that my parents—well, 'minders,' sent me to," Eva said. "Dr. Dark."

Sam looked at her as the helicopter circled around to land at the Academy's mountain-top campus in the Swiss Alps.

"Come again?"

"My parents made me see some dream expert— Dr. Dark."

"No way!"

"What?" Eva said, then made the connection. "Wait, you see the *same* guy?"

"Yes." Sam was dumbstruck.

"And he's Xavier's *father*?" Eva asked in amazement.

"Yep." The cabin rocked as the aircraft touched down next to the medieval building.

"That's . . . that's a big coincidence."

"Too big," Sam said.

"What does it mean?" The door to their helicopter opened before Sam could answer, and they ran across the snow-covered ground to the Academy.

Inside, they headed straight for the Professor's office.

"Sam!"

He turned and saw—

"Lora!" Sam said, as she crashed into him and hugged him so tight he felt as though she'd squeeze his guts out. She let go and he noticed that her arm was in a sling. "Are you OK?"

She nodded. "Just a sprain."

"Hello, Sam," a deep, familiar voice said. "Welcome back."

"Professor!" Sam beamed a smile at him.

"I can't begin to tell you how relieved we all are to see you here," the Professor said, his face as soft and caring as a grandfather's.

"Tell me," Sam said, "when I called you from Cairo, how'd you already know where I was?"

The Professor nodded and gestured across the room. "I had a little help from a friend."

Sam turned to see Lora standing at an open cabinet containing a globe of the earth. It was a big antique one which had little glowing dots dispersed all over its surface.

"But how?" Sam persisted. "How'd you find me?"

"Anyone wearing one of our dream catcher charms can be located on this globe," Lora explained. "It's not an exact science, but if you keep it on it gives us a good starting point when we need to find you."

Sam looked closely at the globe, covered with hundreds of tiny pinpricks of red light, most clustered around the world's major cities.

Sam asked, "What about Alex's?"

Lora shook her head. "It's not working, it might have gotten damaged."

"How did you get from New York to Cairo?" the Professor asked Sam.

He told them about Xavier, keeping his promise not to mention his dream, then about the coincidence of the Enterprise sending him to the same psychiatrist as Eva.

"Yes, I know Dr. Dark well," the Professor said, lost in thought. "He's very good, a wonderfully analytical mind, but as you say, it's a bit too coincidental. I wouldn't put it past him to have all kinds of dealings with all kinds of people over the years."

Sam nodded, unsure what to say. Xavier's father had

been nothing but kind and caring to him over the last year. *Then again, the same could be said of those Agents posing as my parents.*

"Why did you go to Cairo?" Lora asked.

"It seemed like the logical place to start—I'd dreamed of the Star of Egypt, and that's where the Dream Stele is from," Sam said. "It's like I was drawn there."

"And what did you find there?" the Professor said.

"Not what I expected, but perhaps what we needed . . ." Sam said, his hand touching the key under his shirt. "Though I doubted myself when I was being questioned by security guards."

"Security guards?" Eva asked.

"I'll tell you all the boring details later," Sam said, the relief of being safe and amongst friends leading to a wave of exhaustion from the last twenty-four hours of adrenalin-fuelled escapades.

"Do you have any more news on Alex?" Sam asked the Professor.

"We found out that he snuck out of the safe house in Manhattan," Lora sighed. "It's clear that he wanted to help you, Sam—he just couldn't stay away." Lora studied her globe, looking at New York City. She pinched her fingers there and then spread them apart, so that the area zoomed in—it was a digital globe, Sam could see now, like a screen but spherical. Manhattan was full of bright little lights, hundreds of Dreamers milling about, and Lora studied them forlornly, looking for something she knew she wouldn't find.

"Couldn't stay away?" Sam said. "Where was he last?"

"As far as we can work out, he'd made it almost all the way to the café. Then the jet exploded, and we lost the signal. We've got Guardians in the area looking for him now."

"So he was close to the blast?"

Lora nodded.

"Oh . . ." Sam said. He remembered the explosion, the flaming wreck. So massive. "But we don't know for sure, right? I mean, maybe he dropped the dream catcher there or something."

Lora shrugged. "It's possible."

Sam asked, "What about Sebastian?"

"No sign of him either," Lora replied. She looked longingly at the locator globe, turning it absently.

Sam knew that for Sebastian there could be little uncertainty—he'd been inside the plane, and there was surely no chance of anyone surviving that. He could feel the sadness in the room. With Sebastian gone, the Professor had lost a son, Lora her boyfriend, and the Academy students a teacher and friend.

"Professor, I have something to tell you, and Lora," Sam said hesitantly. "About what happened to the jet . . . it—it didn't just crash, or explode. It was attacked."

"It's OK, Sam," the Professor said, his tone calm and

even. "And we know about the rogue Agent in the subway station."

"How did you . . . ?" Sam asked.

"Remember, Sam, we've had Shiva working for us for a while," Lora said. "He told us what happened in the subway station after I got knocked out. About Stella pretending to be Solaris."

"Well, what are we going to do about her?" Sam said. "Do the Enterprise know they have an Agent who's trying to kill us?"

"Trust us, those who need to know, do," the Professor reassured. "We're monitoring the situation. She's revealed herself now, but she doesn't know that Shiva saw her. So for now we wait to find out who else she's working with, and then we can stop her."

"And Tobias?" Sam said, suddenly feeling guilty for not asking about him sooner, the one member of the Academy who'd been in Sam's life for years, masquerading as his teacher at Sam's old school, watching over him.

"We've had no word," the Professor said.

"He's missing?" Sam asked.

"There may be more to it," Lora said, then looked to the Professor as if seeking permission to explain further. "With the attack at the museum by the Egyptian Guardians, we fear that he might also be a part of some bigger conspiracy."

"Tobias? You think he may be a traitor? That's crazy!"

Sam said, wondering how they could possibly consider such a thing. "I mean, didn't his Guardians turn on him too?"

"We have to be careful about all this until we know more," the Professor said. "The Dreamer Council in Paris is already demanding that I hand over you and the rest of the last 13 as they appear, as our security is clearly compromised and there are forces at work that we do not know enough about."

Sam was unsure what to think, but he knew he was mad at the suggestion of Tobias being anything other than a good guy.

"The Council can't take us away from here, can they?" Eva asked.

"I've convinced them for now that this is the most secure place for you," the Professor replied, his bushy eyebrows heavy over his eyes and his reading glasses down low on the tip of his nose. "I don't like this any more than you do, and I really don't believe that Tobias could be caught up in it, but we have every reason to be cautious now."

"But what if they have him?" Sam said. "What if Tobias or Alex are being held captive by these Guardi—traitors? Can't we search for them? Can't we send everyone out there and search?"

"We're doing what we can," Lora said.

"There's too much at stake to take risks," the Professor said. "I'm sorry, Sam, but we must stay focused on this race. We must overcome Solaris, and everyone else. I'll do what I can to keep the Council at bay."

The room was silent. Lora looked at the Professor, who had his back to them, contemplating the vast mountains outside. Sam saw that Lora was angry too, all talked out, and he knew that they all needed to rest. He shifted uncomfortably, his legs and arms still sore from his climb on the pyramid. *Man, I'm hungry.*

"If it's OK," he said, "I think I might go take a shower and have a bite to eat."

"Of course," the Professor said.

"I'll walk with you," Eva said to Sam.

"Oh, Sam?" the Professor said, and Sam turned around. "The Star of Egypt—what became of it?"

"Oh, right!" Sam said, feeling a little embarrassed as he walked back to the Professor, taking off his dream catcher necklace. "Well, I got it. In a sense you could say that I beat Solaris in round one—though that's not entirely true."

"Yes, we must hear all about that," the Professor said, excited, but adding, "later, of course."

"Yeah, right, and, um . . ." Sam took off the key, blew the sandy dust off it, revealing the glinting five-pointed star of gold. "I'm afraid the sapphire didn't make it in one piece."

They all looked at him oddly.

"I mean," Sam explained, "that when I came to at sunrise, I saw the Star just near me on top of the Great Pyramid, and it had, well, broken in half." Sam took the two pieces of the Star of Egypt from his pockets and held them out sheepishly.

"On *top* of the Great Pyramid?" Eva said, behind him.

"Yeah, more to tell you later," Sam said, turning back to the Professor and handing him the key. "I'm really sorry it got broken."

The Professor and Lora studied it closely.

"Interesting . . ." the Professor said. "I think we'll find, Sam, that this key was what was so important about the Star of Egypt."

"Yeah," Sam said. "That's what I've heard."

## ALEX

"**C**are to explain how you came to be in New York?" a detective asked. Two of them stood there, wearing suits with badges clipped onto the breast pockets.

Alex blinked away the confusion. Around him various machines hummed, a heart-rate monitor was connected to his finger and bleeping away, and an IV drip was taped onto his arm.

"Where you from, kid?" the other, younger cop asked.

Alex caught glimpses of doctors and nurses walking by the open door. The younger cop rapped his knuckles on Alex's medical chart. *Why are they questioning me like this? Shouldn't they be investigating that explosion?*

"Better start talkin' . . ."

"Sorry, what?" Alex asked them.

"You were found at the scene of a bombing," the younger cop continued. "So I'd start talking if I were you, kid."

*Bombing?* Alex knew he was in a hospital in New York, but how exactly he came to be there was a blank. He remembered an explosion. *Maybe the trauma messed with my memory? How long have I been here?*

"I—I can't . . ." Alex said, searching for what to say. His head spun. "I don't feel so good."

"The doctors said you're fine," the cop replied. "Why don't you start with a name? Hmm?"

Alex squinted against a searing stabbing pain in his head, there and gone again.

"I'm Detective Montrose and this here," the older, balding man pointed to his colleague with the grin on his face, "is Detective Carter. What can we call you?"

"You've got a lot of scratches on your hands . . ." Detective Carter sniggered to his partner, then turned to Alex with his game face back on. "Means you were right there, at the centre of the blast, though how you managed to survive, I don't know. You must be the luckiest kid alive."

"Who you workin' for?"

Alex shook his head, his mouth open but no answer came out. The detectives looked at one another. One shook his head, the other shrugged.

"Take the easy option here, kid. Start talkin'."

Alex remained silent.

"You were found at the crime scene. Are you affiliated with a terrorist organization?" Montrose asked.

"What?" Alex said, shocked. *They think I'm a terrorist?*

The cops smiled and settled in.

"It's OK, we got nuthin' but time," Carter said. Alex got the feeling that whatever was going to happen, it was going to go from bad to worse.

Montrose sat and read a magazine, Carter played a game on his phone. Neither had spoken for at least an hour. When Alex asked for food, Carter ignored him but Montrose went out and came back with a burger and a soft drink.

*Are they playing "good cop, bad cop?" Really?*

"Thanks," Alex said, munching away.

"How's that memory coming along?" Montrose asked.

"The last thing I remember," Alex said, "was seeing a—"

Before anyone could say another word, the door opened and four people in grey suits entered. Immediately, Alex knew who they were, memories rushing back. *Enterprise Agents!*

"We'll take it from here, detectives," the female Agent said. Her face looked bruised, but no one in the room commented on it. ID was flashed and Montrose shrugged. Carter looked like he was about to argue, when Montrose shook his head with a "why bother" look on his face. Carter responded by giving Alex a smile that said "your life is about to get a lot harder." The detectives left before he could even plead with them to stay.

"So," the woman said, "what did you tell the police?"

Alex shook his head and swallowed hard.

Her eyes flashed brilliant blue as she stared at him.

"Nothing!" Alex said. "I told them nothing!"

The woman continued looking at Alex with an assessing gaze. Satisfied, she inspected his medical chart.

"Good. Now, you're coming with us."

She turned to another Agent who locked the door and lowered the blinds. They put on sunglasses, putting a pair onto Alex too. They felt heavy, more like goggles. A briefcase was opened and they took out a blowtorch and casually cut the bars off the window.

"What? We can't just take the elevator? What *is* it with you people?"

"Here," an Agent said, pulling him out of the bed and clipping a harness around Alex and then to himself. "You're riding down with me."

"No way! This is kidnap—" Alex's protests were muffled as a strong arm came around his neck and a hand went over his mouth.

The five of them were out the window in a heartbeat, and terrifying moments later, Alex's feet touched the ground. When he could force his eyes open again, he noticed the glider components of the Agents' Stealth Suits.

*Wish I'd spotted that before we jumped out of a twelfth-floor window and I had a heart attack.*

He tried to make a run for it—

And felt a dart hit him in the middle of his back.

## SAM

Sam stayed in the locker room shower for close to an hour trying to wash away the things he couldn't forget. Whenever he closed his eyes he had visions of Solaris, dressed in that shimmering full-body suit, complete with the mask, showing only those eyes that seemed to see right into him, into his mind and pulling at his thoughts.

He dried off and dressed, and as he sat down to tie his shoes he heard a familiar voice.

"Hey, Sam. I heard you were back!"

It was Pi, a young student he'd met on his first night at the Academy.

"Hey," Sam said. "What's up?"

"What happened to your phone?" Pi asked, sitting down next to Sam on the bench, studying the phone's shattered screen. It seemed to be barely hanging together at the seams. "Looks like it's toast."

"Got a bit knocked around in New York," Sam said. "Then it did some sightseeing around Cairo."

"Cool! What was it like?" Pi asked.

"What was what like?"

"Your adventure."

"Tiring." Sam tried to laugh. "Wouldn't call it an adventure. More like a nightmare."

"Yeah, well, it's still awesome—everyone's talking about it," Pi said, then he put down the phone and turned serious. It took him a moment to go on, as if he was unsure what to say. "What happened to Sebastian?"

Sam hesitated. "I . . . can I give you the lowdown later?"

Pi looked uneasy.

"Pi, what is it?"

He said in a quiet voice, "There's talk that the Academy jet was shot out of the sky."

Sam nodded.

"That the Enterprise did it."

"We're not sure about that," Sam replied. He stopped himself from saying that the Guardians had turned on those they were sworn to protect.

"And I heard that . . . that, ah, Sebastian was on board the plane, and that Tobias and Alex are still missing."

"Yeah," Sam said.

"So maybe they survived?" he added.

"I saw the plane explode . . ." Sam was silent for a moment as he dried his hair. "We didn't see anyone eject. They think Alex was close to the blast . . . but knowing Alex, he'll have found some way to get out of there . . ."

Pi looked like he was going to cry.

"It'll be alright," Sam said, standing up. "We'll beat the Enterprise and Solaris—and whoever else turns up."

Pi smiled at that.

"We'll win this," Sam said.

Several students came into the locker room, their voices dying down when they saw Sam.

"Hey, Sam," the tallest said. He was a senior, who Sam had seen around the corridors. "We heard about the Egyptian Guardians. Traitors. They'll get theirs."

"Did you see them?" another student asked.

"I saw them blow up the Dream Stele."

The boys shared looks of apprehension that belied their bulk and outward confidence around class.

"I can't believe . . ."

"It is what it is," Sam said.

The tall senior came forward, "My name's Channing. I don't think we've officially met yet." He offered a hand and Sam shook it. "We're *all* in this and we got your back, Sam. Any time, any place."

The boys all murmured in agreement, each coming forward and shaking Sam's hand.

"Thanks, guys," Sam said. "I'm going to need all the help I can get."

He stopped by the door, Pi following close behind him, and he turned around and said to them all, "I'll do the best I can."

"We know you will, Sam," Channing said quietly.

# 13

At dinner, Sam sat next to Eva.

"You're thinking about him," Sam said to her and she put her fork down on her plate of vegetarian lasagne. "Alex, I mean . . ."

"I know who you mean," Eva said, looking up at Sam, her eyes wet with tears. "Yeah, as much as Alex bugged me, and I hardly knew him—I'm really worried sick about him. I hope he's OK."

Everyone at the table picked at their food. Students talked quietly, constantly glancing Sam's way. Clearly they understood that life as they knew it—being here, learning how to deal with their Dreamer abilities—was no longer simple, no longer abstract fun. Things had turned *real* serious, *real* fast.

"Eva? What is it?"

Eva shook her head, then said, "I was *there* . . ." Her voice was as distant as her mind's wanderings. "I was with you in New York and there was nothing I could do to help. *Nothing* . . ."

"Well," Sam said, thinking back to the first time he'd met Eva, when he'd been plucked from school and muscled aboard a helicopter by Enterprise Agents. "You foresaw our meeting and the attack on the helicopter that day."

"And what?" she said. "Alex was at the wrong place at the wrong time—under a jet as it was shot out of the sky. Why did none of the Dreamers here see *that*? What use is it if we can see future events but we can't change them, just hold them off, or worse, do nothing? And what does that mean—that you'll be blown out of the air next?"

"Well, I hope not."

"Maybe I'm a one-trick pony, destined to never foresee anything again," Eva looked at him, tears in her eyes. "What if that was it for me, the only true dream I'll ever have? Yeah, I'm some powerful Dreamer all right."

Sam stared down at his dessert, his appetite gone. Before he could say anything else he noticed conversation had stopped at their table and sensed a presence behind him—it was Lora.

She said, "Sam, Eva, if you could come with me?"

Eva stood up and waited impatiently for Sam to do the same. She seemed glad to be leaving, to be doing something. Sam slowly got to his feet and followed them out. He just wanted to go to bed and sleep, but the days of sleeping half the day away like a regular teenager seemed like a distant memory now.

Sam and Eva sat opposite Lora and the Professor in his office.

"As you know," the Professor said to them, seated in comfy chairs around a stone fireplace full of fiercely crackling logs, "yesterday I went to Paris to meet with the Council of Dreamers." They all nodded. "They're mobilizing all the Dreamers we know of. The entire Council—the best Dreamers from around the world—are working hard to uncover the direction of this race."

Sam shifted in his seat, leaning away from the heat of the fire.

"There's no easy way to say this," the Professor said, "the shock waves it will create will be felt on a global scale. We've already seen things spill over into the wider world."

"Have they seen what's ahead for the last 13 Dreamers?" Lora said, sitting forward in her armchair.

The Professor shook his head.

"But so far the dreams, including my own, suggest this will all unfold very quickly—much faster than anyone had previously thought."

The three of them looked to Sam, who was transfixed by the red-hot embers.

"How, ah, how long do we have?" Sam asked.

"Not long enough," the Professor replied, "from your first dream . . . weeks, maybe a few months at the most."

"So—that's it for all thirteen Dreamers?" Sam said.

"Well, twelve, now," the Professor said. "Yes."

Lora looked sickened by the news. "It's not enough time to plan, to make sure we win," she said. "I mean, if this is what we've been waiting centuries for—"

"It's the hand we have been dealt," the Professor said firmly. "The Council confirmed the worst about the Enterprise," the Professor continued, crouched down in front of the flames. "Since the Academy's founding, they have been there—skeptical of us, watching us, studying us. Where we've wanted to teach, they've wanted to exploit. But we've always had an understanding of peace between us."

"What's changed?" Lora asked. "I thought those who attacked us were a part of a rogue element."

"They likely were. But the Enterprise is still a competitor in this race, and they know the stakes have been raised," the Professor said. He looked across to Sam. "They know about your dream."

Sam recalled how he'd overheard his "parents" calling in the details of his nightmare about Solaris. They were really Enterprise Agents, surrogate parents who'd raised him, watching him, waiting for the day he'd have *that* dream. Sam was still torn between wanting to question them and missing them.

"So they want to capture as many of the last 13 as they can?" Eva asked.

"That's how I understand it," the Professor said slowly. "The Enterprise collected DNA from leading Dreamers in the past and used it to create potential Dreamers like you.

They hoped to increase their chances of having control of the last 13 when the prophecy was realized."

"But nature, and true dreaming, can't be so easily manipulated and contained," Lora added. "Genetically-engineered Enterprise children never reached their Dreaming potential when brought up in a controlled setting. Which is why they went to elaborate lengths to put potential Dreamers in a natural environment so they could flourish. Hence, the parents you had and the families that you grew up in."

"So do the Enterprise know who all of the last 13 Dreamers will be?" Eva asked.

"I don't think they do. I don't think anyone does yet," the Professor replied. "But I'll wager that they won't all be Enterprise-controlled Dreamers. This prophecy is far too powerful to be reduced to a mere lottery. I believe many of the 13 will be naturally occurring Dreamers, without any clue of what their dreams will mean, and with no one to report them to the Enterprise."

"That's why they want me. I'm the one who will lead them to the rest of the 13," Sam said. "I'm right, aren't I, Professor?"

The Professor nodded, and there was silence between them, the only noise the crackle of the fire.

## ALEX

"**A**rgh!" Alex pulled the black hood off his face.

He was seated in the back of a big SUV, his wrists bound. The female Enterprise Agent now sat up front in the passenger seat, while two Agents sat opposite Alex in the back—one with a dart gun levelled squarely at Alex's chest.

He looked over his shoulder as they tore out of the hospital's parking lot.

"Wait!" Alex said. "Where are you taking me?"

No one replied. The driver took to the streets with the fervour of a rally driver. Alex felt groggy from the dart. The world outside flashed by in a blur.

"You're from the Enterprise, aren't you?" Alex said.

No answer.

"Who are you?"

No answer.

*Please, just tell me . . .*

The female Agent turned around, annoyed. Now he looked closer, her face looked like she'd gone a few rounds in the boxing ring—black eye and fat lip, swollen nose.

"My name is Stella," she said in a clipped tone. "And yes, I work for the Enterprise."

"What are you going to do with me?"

"We're here to help you," she replied.

"Yeah, right. As if." Alex couldn't keep the sarcasm out of his voice.

*What am I doing? Shut up, idiot! Don't make them angry.* Stella shrugged.

"Where are you taking me?" he said, trying for a more even tone.

She looked to her driver. "Somewhere safe."

*Yeah, I bet, real safe.* This felt all wrong. Alex knew he'd probably be far safer back at the hospital with the cops, even if they did think he was some kind of terrorist.

They ground to a halt in traffic. The lights changed but they moved only a few metres. Up front, Stella talked on a phone, distracted . . .

*Now or never.*

Alex reached across the Agent to his left and grabbed for the door handle, ready to shove the Agent out before him with all his strength. The door seemed locked at the first pull, but as he yanked it again it clicked open. He shoved hard against the Agent and they both spilled out of the door—

"Argh!" Alex felt a stabbing pain in his neck, followed by the familiar warm, fuzzy feeling. He turned to see

Stella holding her dart gun at point-blank range, feeling the sting of the little barbed dart still in his neck.

*Not again . . .*

He was powerless to stop the now disgruntled Agent from shoving him back onto the seat and heard the doors *clunk* as they were re-locked. Stella shook her head and muttered something to herself, but he couldn't make it out as he slipped into unconsciousness once more.

## EVA

"**W**e need to examine your dream from Cairo," the Professor said to Sam, as they and Eva walked down through the lower levels of the Academy.

Eva looked over to Sam and could see he seemed pleased to be visiting Jedi once more. He told Eva that he'd liked the Academy's technology wizard instantly when he'd first met him in his computer lab. As they walked deeper into the mountain, Eva marvelled at the maze of tunnels dug out from the solid rock.

"I didn't get to come down here last time, this is seriously cool," she said as they passed door after door—some showing large empty rooms, some full of intriguing shapes shrouded in tarpaulins, others occupied by teachers and students.

"If you think this is cool, wait till you meet Jedi," Sam whispered as they came around the last corner to Jedi's lab. As they walked in, the room was buzzing with the hum of the computers that stretched from one end of the long room to the other. Jedi waved to them from his glass office and they headed straight in.

"Nice to see you back with us, Sam," Jedi said as he spun around in his chair to greet them. "And this must be Eva."

"Great to meet you, Dr. Jedko," Eva said.

"Please, call me Jedi." Jedi was all smiles. "So, whose dream are we tapping into today?"

"Sam has potentially dreamed of the next of the last 13," the Professor said. "So we'll take a closer look and see if we can pinpoint who it is, or at least glean as much information as we can."

"Sure thing, just give me a second to set things up," Jedi replied, immediately busying himself with all kinds of mysterious gadgets. "Feel free to take a look around while you wait," he waved expansively around the cluttered room.

"I might also need to hit you up for some phone repairs," Sam smiled as Jedi adjusted dials and levers at a control panel.

"This is going to be a bad habit with you, I can just tell," Jedi joked, giving the wrecked phone a quick once over. "But the good news is I've got a new toy for you this time—a portable machine so you can replay dreams when you don't have access to my awesomeness in person. I'll show you how to work it later. Try not to break it."

He and Sam laughed together.

*Sam's definitely met a kindred spirit down here.* Eva tried not to smile as she looked around Jedi's office. Books and boxes of computer pieces littered every available surface, while empty soft drink cans and a stack of food trays surrounded a trundle bed in one corner.

"This guy *lives* down here?" she said to herself under her breath.

Sam walked over to gaze at Jedi's impressive wall of screens embedded in the far wall. There had to be at least fifty, all showing different channels—foreign news stations, weather reports, IT headlines, even old movies and music videos. Just as he turned away, one screen near the bottom caught his eye. He leaned closer.

"Are you OK, Sam?" Eva asked, joining him in front of the screens. "You look like you've seen a ghost."

Sam silently pointed.

"Sam? Sam, you're scaring me now, what is it?" Eva asked, grabbing hold of his arm and giving him a gentle shake. The Professor and Jedi stopped their conversation.

Sam turned to them all.

"I don't think we'll need the dream machine today, Jedi," Sam said as they all looked on, incredulous. "The search is already over." He pointed again. On the screen, a music video played, showing a young girl dancing in the street, all trendy clothes and back-up dancers. "We just need to figure out who *that* is."

"Well, that's not going to be hard," Eva said sarcastically. She looked at the three of them and saw that they weren't getting it at all. "Wait—none of you *recognize* her?"

They all leaned in to stare at the image on the screen.

"Right, I forgot you're not teenage girls," Eva said. "Her name is Gabriella."

"Seriously?" Sam said, taking a closer look. "So it is . . ."

"You *know* her?" Jedi said.

"Know *of* her," Eva replied. Sam nodded in agreement.

"So, who is she?" Jedi asked.

"Gabriella," said Eva, "is an Italian pop singer. She's sold like a billion albums in less than a year. And, according to Sam, she is apparently also one of the last 13."

"Well, I don't know about how many albums she's sold, but she's the girl from my dream, that's for sure," Sam said.

"Wow," said Jedi. He turned to his keyboard, googling for pages on the singer. "Yep, that's Gabriella . . . lives in Rome."

"Can you remember anything about how you meet her?" the Professor asked Sam. "We can use the dream machine to find that out, and for other details that may be helpful in changing the course of events."

"I remember looking down from a balcony and there was a crowd of people and a huge cake," Sam said.

"Like a birthday cake, maybe?" Jedi asked, tapping away on his keyboard. "Looks like Gabriella is about to turn sixteen and she's going to celebrate." He spun his screen around to show them a recent article from a celebrity gossip website.

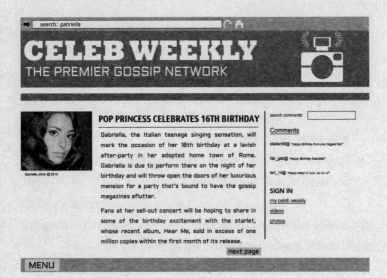

next page

"Good work, Joe," the Professor said. "We're obviously on the right track. Lora will speak to our best contact in Italy and we'll find out how to get Sam into her birthday party. Leave it with us."

"In the meantime, we need to take a closer look at that dream, Sam," Jedi grinned. "Take a seat and we'll go for a spin in your subconscious."

## ALEX

"**A**re you going to kill me?"

"No," Stella said.

"But this is the Enterprise," Alex argued. "You experiment on Dreamers like me."

"Are you sure that's what you are?" she sneered.

"I'm—I want to leave, now. Take me back to the hospital in New York."

She moved her hand toward her holstered dart gun. "I can always get this out again, if you like?"

Alex fell silent. He sat on a chair in the middle of the room. He had no idea where he was—he'd come to just a minute ago, waking to find himself in a non-descript room, with this "Stella" for company.

*What's with me getting kidnapped all the time? I've gotta get out of here.*

The door slid open and a middle-aged man strode confidently into the room, tall and still youthful in his features. His thick, greying hair was brushed back in a slick style, his clothes casual but obviously expensive and well tailored. He wore a pair of sharp glasses that somehow made him look smarter. But it was his prosthetic left arm—a very realistic, high-grade prosthetic—that really caught Alex's attention.

"Good, he's your problem now," Stella said and left without another word.

The man nodded to her as she left, then turned to Alex. "Hello," he said, smiling. "My name is Jack."

Alex looked at the outstretched hand offered in greeting and ignored it.

"Are you feeling OK?"

Alex said nothing.

"Can I get you a drink, something to eat?" Jack persisted.

Alex tried to ignore his dry throat.

Jack put a bag on the table in front of Alex.

"That's a change of clothes," he said. "I'll wait outside the door, come out when you're ready and we'll go to the cafeteria."

He left the room, the door shutting automatically behind him.

Alex moved fast. He changed out of his hospital gown and into the jeans and T-shirt provided, which, like the cool sneakers, were exactly his size. He scanned the room—there were no windows, nothing but the door and an air vent in the ceiling. He stood on the table and tried to pull the cover off. It was screwed on tight.

"Are you OK in there?" Jack called.

Alex jumped off the table and went over to the door.

*I've got no choice but to play along for now.*

He rapped on the door and it slid back at the touch of Jack's security card. Alex stepped out cautiously and found himself standing in the middle of a big open space, full of shiny workstations and blinking screens. The busy office looked like both an IT hub and a science lab. At least thirty people bustled about, checking screens and speaking into headsets.

"Come, follow me," Jack said, motioning toward an open doorway. "This way."

Alex hesitated then followed him. Through the doorway, they came out into blinding sunshine. Alex shaded his eyes against the glare and noticed the lenses in Jack's glasses turn dusky brown. *I thought we were inside?*

Alex looked up and saw a domed roof far above him, blue sky and clouds drifting past high overhead. As he gazed all around him, Alex realized he was in the large atrium of a high-rise building. Far below him were many levels of similar offices, all giving out onto the central space, lit so spectacularly from above. At the bottom, Alex could just make out shady palm trees and a fountain in the centre of the ground floor.

"What is this place?" he asked, in awe.

Jack spread his arms out to take in the modern architectural grandeur around them. "*This* is the Enterprise headquarters."

## SAM

Sam scratched at his mess of hair, sand still falling out of it, and sat with Eva in the lounge at the end of their dorm floor. Most students had gone to bed, but the curfew didn't seem to be rigidly enforced. An open fire crackled before them and bathed them in a warm orange glow. Sam sat away from it, just close enough to catch the heat. He could tell that Eva noticed his apprehension.

"That dream was intense," she said. "It doesn't have to end that way, you know."

"Yeah," he said, sipping a hot drink. "Don't have much choice though, do I?"

"What do you mean?"

"I have to do this," he said. "It was my dream that started this race and now it looks like I'm responsible for finding the next of the last 13, maybe more."

"Well, at least you *have* a role."

Sam looked at her. "You're part of this too."

"I doubt it." Eva leaned her head against the back of the

chair, staring vacantly at the fire.

"You are," Sam said. "You had that dream with me in it. Just trust that you'll have more."

"We'll see," Eva replied, and hesitated. "Sam, you have a *choice*—you *always* have a choice, you know that, right?"

"Yeah, I know. It's just—I can't just sit this one out. And now what? I'm supposed to meet this famous pop star and say, 'Hey, don't suppose you've had a strange dream recently? You're supposed to help me save the world. How about it?'"

Eva laughed, then Sam did too, nearly snorting out a mouthful of his drink.

"And I'll have to go with her, get chased by teams of Agents, and run through stacks of dusty books toward what's sure to be a nasty end. Again."

"Just don't choose that tunnel on the right," Eva said.

Sam laughed. "Maybe I have to."

"You don't!" Eva leaned over and punched him in the arm. "You can change it, bonehead. You should see the dream as an example of what *not* to do."

"And just put off my impending death?"

"We all check out someday, maybe you'll put yours off for decades—hey, you might be a hundred and then die of old age while some geriatric Agents chase you on walkers through a retirement home."

Sam smiled but it faded fast. "That's assuming we succeed, and win this race . . ."

Time passed where neither of them spoke before Eva looked up at Sam, determination in her eyes. "I'm coming with you."

"OK," Sam said, sitting on the edge of his chair and considering this new development. "But you weren't in my dream."

"Good," she said, "then we're starting to change it already."

"Good point. You might need to convince Lora, though."

"I will," she smiled.

"Huh." He put his mug down on the side table.

"What?" she said.

He shook his head, reminiscing. "My mom—I mean—ah . . ." he stalled, before trying again, "the Enterprise Agent who raised me, used to make the best hot chocolate. My dad used to try to make it too, but it never tasted the same." Sam smiled at the memory, lost in an unfocused stare at the wall. "He'd put it on but then forget about it, and the whole house would smell like burnt milk for days. Mom would go ballistic."

Eva said, "I know what you mean. I get that they turned out to be Enterprise Agents, but they totally still feel like my mom and dad. I miss them."

"Do you think maybe it wasn't all an act?" Sam asked. "That they really cared for us?"

"Maybe," Eva said. "I don't know."

"But they were working for the Enterprise the whole time . . ." Sam trailed off.

"All I know was that I always felt loved. If it was just an act, then someone should give them an award or something, because it was the performance of a lifetime."

They both returned to silently watching the crackling fire, each thinking about the lives they would never return to.

Lora walked in, carrying some notebooks. She looked at Sam and Eva, seeing from their expressions that they had been discussing something personal.

"It's hard, what you're going through, getting used to such a dramatic change in your lives," Lora said. "And I can't imagine how tough it's been for you, Sam. You've gone straight from finding out you're a Dreamer to being part of the last 13. But, it will get easier for you both, especially when you fully understand what you can achieve through your dreams."

"Will we learn to dream deeper?" Eva asked.

"You'll learn to remember every little detail, and even re-enter your dream in waking life, to explore it further."

"Cool," Eva said.

"Really?" Sam said. "I don't know if that is cool. I'd rather not know that death's waiting around the corner for me."

"Well," Lora said, "in the meantime, you get these—old school."

She passed them both a pad and pen.

"Serious?"

"Dream journals," she explained.

"I know," Sam said, "my 'parents' made me keep one of these."

"Take notes about your dreams," Lora said, "and as you inspect them, you'll start to drive them more and more—you can train yourself to pay closer attention to the parts that are important and have a greater awareness when you're in a dream."

Sam said, "Like when I went back into my dream earlier, I already knew it was a dream and it was like I was watching myself in the third person, like in a movie."

"Actually, that's a good description of it, and you'll learn more in your dreaming lessons with Professor Bauer, which I had hoped you'd be starting today." Lora stood and walked to the window. She remained silent and still, watching something outside.

"What is it?" Eva asked.

They joined her. The view outside was nothing but darkness, the empty mountains hidden by the light in the room reflected on the glass.

The room suddenly fell dark and Eva jumped in shock.

"Sorry, I should have warned you I was going to do that," Lora said, her hand moving from the control panel that shielded the fire with a steel cover and turned off the lights. Once their eyes had adjusted, the sky outside was a blanket of stars. She pointed to a spot among the mountains. "Watch closely."

Without the glow of the fire and lamps in the room,

details emerged in the landscape outside, lit by the half moon.

At first, Sam could see nothing but craggy, cold, desolate mountains.

"There!" Lora said.

"I saw it too!" Sam chorused.

"What? Where?" Eva asked.

"A dot of light," Sam said.

"Like a campfire . . ." Lora said, looking out at the scene with binoculars. "It's the glow of a fire, perhaps at the mouth of a cave."

They stood and watched but the light had disappeared.

"Who do you think it is?"

"Not sure," Lora said, turning around. Their room came to life with lights and the warm fire again. "I could swear someone was out there, watching us."

"But there's barely anything to make a fire with," Sam said. "Surely no one could survive out there? Not for long, anyway."

"It's too dark to investigate now. I'll ask the Guardians to take a look in the daylight. We can't be too careful at this point," Lora said. "But now it's time to get some sleep, we have a lot ahead of us."

The three went their separate ways, and Sam couldn't stop thinking about who might be out there in the freezing mountains, warmed only by a campfire.

## ALEX

"So, these people are all Enterprise Agents?" Alex asked, tucking into his third burrito in the Enterprise cafeteria. He was starting to relax, in spite of himself.

"Some are," Jack said. "Some are field Agents, others work here at our main office—we have about five thousand staff around the globe. This is our main operations centre here in Silicon Valley. Our research labs are in Salinas."

"Dress code is pretty casual," Alex noted.

"We like to blend in, except when it's necessary to stand out."

Alex took another mouthful and said, "What's your role?"

"I'm the Director."

"So—you're in charge of everyone, then?"

"In a sense," he said, drinking his coffee. Everything about this place, including Jack and his techno arm, seemed to be a step ahead of anything Alex had ever encountered.

"So," Alex said, pushing his empty plate away. "Why am I here? I can't stay, you know—the Academy are probably desperate to know where I am."

"They know you're here, Alex. I told the Professor the moment you arrived."

"Oh, right," Alex said, cracking his knuckles. "So Lora and a team are on their way, I guess. There's not going to be another bust-up is there?"

"No, not exactly," Jack said, smiling at the notion. "Alex, no one's coming to pick you up—at least, not for now. They said they would be in contact if and when they needed you." Jack paused, watching closely, seeing the disappointment spread on Alex's face. "I think you'll find that the Academy's priority right now is Sam. The rest, including you, is secondary."

Alex's face burned red, like he'd just been slapped.

Jack looked at him and smiled sympathetically. "Come on, let me show you around."

A few moments later, Alex stood at the rail of the mezzanine and looked around the huge room. About a hundred or so Agents were sitting at work consoles. Each of the four walls was covered with a large screen.

"What is this place?" Alex asked.

"It's where we make sure the world keeps turning. The Professor's school does some good, I'm sure, but—"

"But you think you can do better?"

"In a sense, yes, I do."

"Do you want to get rid of all the Dreamers?" Alex asked, taking a small step back.

"No, we don't, not at all," Jack said, a little exasperated

but still smiling. "In fact, far from it. Come, I'll show you something else."

As Alex walked slowly down a bright corridor with Jack he could see a coloured reflection around him, just like he saw in the glass walkway at the Academy.

"Is this reading my Dreamer abilities?" Alex asked, following Jack.

"Abilities?" Jack asked, pausing at the end of the corridor.

"How my dreams come true."

"Your dreams have come true?" Jack asked innocently.

"Well, not yet, exactly . . ." Alex stammered.

"Don't worry," Jack said, leading the way. "I'm sure it's not for lack of trying. You can do more than you realize, and we'll show you how."

The automatic doors hissed open and they entered a massive rec room. There were at least twenty or thirty teenagers playing computer and console games, chess, air hockey and table tennis.

"They're Dreamers, just like you," Jack said. "So you can see, we want to learn from you. Nothing sinister here."

Alex had to admit to himself that everyone seemed to be having a great time.

"So I *will* have true dreams?" he asked.

"When you dream, we can analyze it; but we have far superior technology than the Academy's rather quaint dream machines," Jack laughed.

"And that means?" Alex persisted.

"We can find out what you can do. But you're even more unique than the others."

"How unique?" Alex raised an eyebrow, suddenly interested.

"OK, one more thing to show you. This way."

As Alex looked around, the idea of hanging out and playing some computer games, just being a normal guy for a while, was achingly appealing.

He reluctantly turned and followed Jack from the room.

"Wow," Alex said.

"I know," Jack said.

Alex watched the footage again—amateur video of the Academy's jet coming in to hover over the Manhattan streets. The hot plume of the missile streaked up and *KLAPBOOM*—an explosion, a fireball.

"That was your missile!" Alex accused.

"No," Jack said. "It wasn't us—we don't do that, we're not killers."

Alex eyed Jack carefully. *Hmm, OK, I'll take that, for now.*

"We're making our own inquiries into who shot down the aircraft," Jack continued, then adjusted the controls to replay the footage. "OK, here, watch this area."

Alex saw the image Jack was pointing to, now in extreme slow motion—there was a person, running toward the jet and then ducking behind a car a split second before the explosion radiated overhead.

"That's me, right?" Alex couldn't stop staring at the screen. *How did I know to do that?*

"You were protected by the car. It's like you *knew* to be right there, right then. You foresaw it."

Jack replayed the recording again—the explosion of the aircraft and the slow motion debris falling down, down then hitting the car. His survival had been nothing short of a miracle of timing.

Alex worked a kink out of his neck. "You're saying, *what*? What does that prove?"

"You dreamed it," Jack said. "You dreamed where to be at that exact moment and you acted on that. And by your obvious surprise, I'm guessing you didn't even know it. We can show you how to harness your dreams and the insight they give you. You obviously have a gift—you have a right to be able to use it. It's not just all about Sam."

Alex watched the screen. "I thought Sebastian was a Dreamer too. How come he ended up . . . you know . . . ?"

"He didn't see it coming. Very unfortunate and unlucky," Jack sighed. He continued to watch the explosion on replay. "The Professor's son . . ." Jack said, mostly to himself, "so much is changing, so fast."

Jack snapped out of his thoughts and leaned forward in his chair to turn off the monitor. He swivelled around to face Alex, fingers tapping softly on the armrest.

"I think you *know* you have a gift, Alex. Think about it," Jack paused, before continuing, "when you were growing up, did you ever have the feeling that you could do things others couldn't? That you were somehow different, in a good way?"

Alex thought for a moment, running back over the last few years in his mind. There were times he could remember when he sensed he just knew stuff, more than other people—like he could be in control and completely on top of things.

*Is that a gift? If it is, maybe the Enterprise is the place for me . . .*

"It's up to you, Alex," said Jack, holding Alex's stare, "you're old enough now to be deciding your own fate without being restricted by classrooms and rules. It comes down to whether you want to sit back and wait for life to happen to you, or whether you want to be in on the action. Whether you want to be a leader or follower. If you want to lead, then you're in the right place."

## 19

**SAM**

Eva and Lora walked across the tarmac with Sam. He fumbled with his phone, trying to find some music to help him stay relaxed. He gave up on the distraction. Behind them strode three big Guardians—a moving wall of muscle.

"Any news on Alex or Tobias?" Sam asked.

"I'm sorry," Lora sighed. "We just can't find them. It's like they've both vanished."

Sam nodded. He knew they were doing everything they could. He looked back over to the Guardians behind them. "And you're sure we can trust them?" he asked out of the side of his mouth as he fell into step with Lora.

"I'm sure. Those traitors in New York were Egyptian Guardians," she replied. "The rest of the Guardians are beyond reproach."

"But—"

"They'll get to the bottom of why they turned," she explained. "We've got teams tracking them down and all the Guardians here are lining up to punch them in the face when they do." Lora paused mid-stride and asked Sam,

"Why are you walking funny?"

"It's these shoes, they're uncomfortable," Sam replied. In the blink of an eye, Lora changed his shoes.

"*They're* made from that stealth fabric too?" Sam asked in amazement.

The pilot signalled to Lora that the helicopter was ready for boarding. As they got in, the helicopter's rotors started to turn slowly, winding up for takeoff. A soft hum radiated out over the mountain top.

"All the material used in your clothing is the same type," Lora said. "Once you learn how to control it, the possibilities are endless—and it sure saves on wardrobe space."

"I feel a bit underdressed," Sam said to them, looking at his friends in their cool outfits—Eva was dressed in something that looked like it came from a high-fashion runway—and then down at his own jeans and hoodie.

Eva leaned over and whispered something to Lora, who laughed and nodded.

"What's so funny?" Sam asked as he buckled in and the helicopter took off. "Argh!" His clothes changed appearance. Eva held up her phone, showing a picture of an annoying teen movie star, whose outfit he now wore. "Really, that guy? Eurgh."

"Hey, he has better taste in clothes than you do," Eva said, chuckling.

Sam shuffled to get comfortable in his seat, nervously fingering the dream catcher strap around his neck. He'd managed to persuade the Professor to let him keep the key with him on his trip to Rome. "I don't know why, but I just know I need it. I guess maybe its purpose is buried in my dream somewhere," he'd told the Professor.

Now with Guardians on either side of him, he hoped the key would be safe. His two friends and the third Guardian sat opposite. Before Sam could complain again, his shoes changed into a comfortable pair like those he would have worn back home. "Thanks, Eva. You're really going to have to teach me how to do that."

"I will, but these don't go with your outfit now," Eva said.

"What!" Sam mimed mock horror. "Yeah, well," he said, smiling down at his shoes, "whatcha gonna do?"

Sam's shoes changed again, this time to some cool, black boots that actually fit fine.

"Thanks for that, Lora," Sam said, "but please stop—both of you. I can't believe I'm the only one who can't do that yet and you're fast becoming the two annoying sisters I never had."

At Geneva airport, a small private jet was waiting on the tarmac.

Lora smiled to the pilots as they climbed aboard. The Guardians sat up front, silent and stony-faced, while the Dreamers sat together toward the rear of the plane.

"How long's the flight?" Sam asked.

"We'll be in Rome before sundown," Lora replied.

Already the aircraft was moving fast down the runway.

"And how am I getting into this party?" Sam asked, thinking back to his dream, which began there.

"Ta-da!" Lora said, handing over an ID with Sam's photo on it. "This is your press pass. You'll be posing as a reporter, with backstage access to her concert. The Enterprise aren't the only ones with ways and means of getting things done."

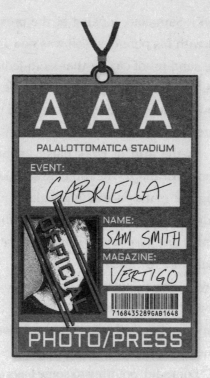

"Gabriella has a show tonight," Eva explained. "Her birthday's something of an after-party."

"When you get backstage, you'll have ten minutes after the gig to do a scheduled interview with Gabriella," Lora added.

"So, let me get this straight," Sam said. "I have ten minutes to convince her that she's going to have special dreams that will come true and that she's part of a race in which she will help save the world?"

"Yep."

"Great, OK," Sam said, looking at the press pass, and pocketing it with his phone, which was now in its special shock-proof, sand-proof casing thanks to Jedi. He looked over to Lora, who was studying maps of Rome with Eva.

"You should look over these too," Lora said to him. "The more prepared you are, the better."

Sam sat on the arm of Eva's plush leather seat and looked at one of the maps. The route he and Gabriella took when fleeing the mansion was highlighted, mapped out from his earlier session in Jedi's dream machine. *The city is a maze of streets and alleyways, I doubt I can be sure to take the same route twice. Or avoid it.*

"It's funny, seeing a route that you're *going* to take in a snap decision while being chased," Eva said.

"Just thinking about all this makes my head hurt," he said. "Anyone else hungry?"

"In there," Lora said, pointing to some bags on an empty

seat. "Can't have you fading away on us."

"Thanks," Sam said, chomping through a sandwich.

He sat next to Eva and turned his attention back to the mission at hand.

"OK, let's figure this out," he said through a mouthful.

"Gross," Eva said, watching him eat. "You're like the always-eating annoying brother I never had."

**ALEX**

"**C**ome on, we'll grab a drink," Jack said. He looked at Alex as they walked. "Can you forget whatever you've previously heard about the Enterprise?"

"What," Alex replied, "that you kidnap Dreamers?"

"Now, where would you hear a story like that?" he quizzed.

Alex didn't need to answer.

"I assure you," Jack said, "what we do here is quite the opposite of what you've been told. We just make sure that you reach your full potential."

Alex didn't know whether to believe this guy. He'd only recently, and reluctantly, come around to believing what he had been told by the Academy.

*Who's to say who is right?*

They walked back through the busy games room, and Alex noticed two movie theatres at the end of the hall.

*Cool place to work . . .*

They walked out to a big room with an artificial grass playing field where a loud game of football was underway. Jack led them to some chairs by a café counter. Alex ordered a milkshake from the extensive menu.

"OK, say I believe you," Alex said, and he noticed that Jack was smiling before he'd even said it. "What is it you want with Dreamers?"

"We're here to learn from you," Jack said. "It's a unique set of skills you have. Like I said, it's a gift and the purpose of the Enterprise is to explore that to—"

"To the full, yeah, I got that."

"Right. Well, we like to think of it as enhancing human potential, Alex. We take destiny and we drive it, steer it along its course—but we also like to use the accelerator, so to speak."

Alex nodded at Jack, smiling at his analogy.

"There's nothing wrong in investing in the future," Jack said, "and recognizing the true value of the knowledge and information we can acquire."

Alex found himself still nodding along in agreement, but then frowned. "But, hang on a second—so in order to get this knowledge and information and whatever, that makes it OK to go around kidnapping people or creating dreams or trying to control whatever you like?"

"All we create is possibility, Alex. We are in the business of manufacturing opportunity. Simple as that."

"Right . . . so, say I stay," Alex said. "What is it you want with *me*?"

"You have so much to contribute," Jack said. "It's all very well to have the ability to true dream, and to see things and know of things others cannot grasp. But we consider it a terrible waste to keep these gifts hidden away. They need to be *used*, traded in the real world—in commerce, industry, finance, science, government. The sky really is the limit for you."

Alex gave Jack a long stare. "So why bring me here? Why go to all the trouble?"

Jack sighed, but still he smiled. "Alex, if you really want to leave, you're free to go at any time. It's up to you—you can do what you want . . . but there's someone here who I think you should meet first."

"*Mom?*" Alex felt faint as the blood drained from his cheeks.

Phoebe, the woman Alex had known his whole life as his mother, entered the room and rushed over to him.

"Are you OK?" Phoebe asked, hugging him tightly.

"Yeah," he replied, breaking free from her embrace. There was an awkward silence between them.

"I'm sorry," Phoebe said at last.

"For what?" he said. "Pretending to be my real mother? They told me at the Academy all about the Enterprise trying to create Dreamers, and what I am and who you guys are."

She shook her head, her face sadder than he'd ever seen, and she reached out to put her hand on his face.

"Alex, *please*—I *am* your mother. Your real, biological mother. I would never have agreed to be involved with the Enterprise if I didn't think they would look after us."

He shook his head and felt sick in the stomach.

"I haven't been completely honest with you," she explained, "but surely you can see why. I was *protecting* you."

Alex shook his head again in disbelief. "No. You lied to me. My whole life, you lied to me. And now I find out that you work *here!* You're one of *them!*"

"Please, son—I love you . . ."

"What else did you lie to me about?" Alex said, moving a pace back from her reach. "Dad?"

"Well, no, but—" she stopped herself and looked around the empty room. "It's complicated. A long story."

Alex swallowed hard. "Was he really my dad?"

"No, technically he wasn't." She sighed.

He believed her now that she'd said it like that.

"So," Alex said, looking at his mother, "that story you told me when I was, like, ten, about my father . . ."

"*Is* completely true," Phoebe replied. "My husband died while mountain climbing. And I wanted to have a child, as we'd always planned to—"

"So you had IVF or whatever," Alex finished for her.

Phoebe nodded.

"But you didn't do it the way other people do, did you?" Alex said. "You were part of some special genetics program, where you'd have a baby that was some kind of freak, and that one day you'd just hand him over like an unwanted pet."

"Alex . . ."

Alex said nothing more, only continued to stare at his mother.

"You're gifted, not a freak. And yes, I knew, because I'd been working at the Enterprise for over ten years by then."

"Like your husband?" Alex added.

"Yes," Phoebe said, her eyes welling with tears as she remembered. "You and he would have gotten along so well," she said. "He always wanted to be out in the world, having an adventure, pushing himself, doing new things, taking risks."

"Like climbing Everest?"

"He was attempting to do the Seven Summits," Phoebe said, "one on each of the seven continents. He only had Vinson Massif in Antarctica left after that one . . ."

Alex had read the travel journals of the man he had always thought of as his father, years earlier, and he'd been fascinated by his adventures.

"And his name was Alexander," Alex said.

His mother nodded.

"And that's why you called me Alex?"

"Yes," Phoebe said, wiping her eyes and then looking at him. "I'm so sorry it had to be like this. I was waiting until I thought you were old enough to understand—old enough to cope with it, when I wouldn't have to worry about you anymore."

"How old is that?" Alex asked.

"Oh, I don't know," Phoebe said, gently putting an arm around his shoulders. "How about when I'm ninety?"

They both smiled.

## SAM

The sound inside the PalaLottomatica Stadium was louder than anything Sam had ever heard—and this was just the crowd getting started as they waited for Gabriella to *appear*. Fifteen thousand fans, teenage girls for the most part, all cheering and screaming as they waited between the warm-up act and the main show. He had an earpiece tucked into his left ear but there was little chance of hearing Lora and Eva on the other end.

His two friends waited in a car outside, with three Guardians on motorbikes alongside them, and two more Italian Guardians now in the crowd within, all ready to move at a moment's notice should Sam need to escape.

He made his way through the thronging masses and showed his press pass to security near the stage. He was led to the closest balcony with backstage access for after the show.

"OK, I may already be dead because this is my idea of hell," Sam said into his mic as the amassed crowd began chanting for their pop idol. "I can't hear myself think, let alone hear whatever you guys are saying, but know this—if

I do die tonight, I should be decorated as a hero by the Academy for going well above and beyond the call of duty."

Sam couldn't tell if his bravado was appreciated on the other end. But he knew there wasn't any joke in the world now that could stem his rising nerves.

A buzz of hysteria erupted at movement on the stage. Gabriella's band came out, and when Sam thought it couldn't get any louder, an ear-splitting shriek went up as the star herself made her entrance via a zip line from the back of the stadium.

*It's showtime. For both of us.*

Sam stood up from his seat with the rest of the crowd, girls all around him going berserk in anticipation. It wasn't until halfway through Gabriella's first number that it quietened down enough to actually hear the music. Sam realized then that he'd heard the song on the radio before and that he quite liked it. *Well, it's not bad, but not something I'd choose to listen to for a couple of hours. And I'd rather it wasn't the last song I ever hear. No offence, Gabriella.*

At the mid-show break, Sam made his way backstage.

Gabriella was nowhere to be seen but there was the hurried activity of a few dozen support staff running around helping to get the dancers and musicians changed and ready.

He found a quiet corner and spoke into his mic. "Hello? Anybody there?"

"We hear you. We've got you, Sam," Lora said.

"Any sign of Enterprise Agents?" he said.

"Nothing yet," she said. "We've got a couple of teams of Guardians mobile in the city, watching known Enterprise sites, and Jedi's back at base monitoring security feeds from the airports, so we can hopefully get a heads-up when they make their move."

"Well, we know that they crash the party at some stage . . ." Sam stopped talking as Gabriella and her entourage passed by. She made eye contact as she walked past Sam. *Man, she's amazing! I don't remember that from my dream.*

"Sam, you still there?" Lora said.

"Um, yeah."

"What's wrong?" she asked.

"Nothing."

"Did you just see Gabriella?" Eva guessed.

"Maybe." Sam sounded sheepish.

"Ha!" Eva said. "Getting a bit starstruck, are you?"

"No," Sam said, a bit too quickly. He watched Gabriella go upstairs, but before she disappeared she looked back his way once again. "OK, maybe, a little bit."

"Well, if it's any consolation, I've never met anyone famous either," Eva replied.

"I'll try to keep my head," Sam said. "Gotta go, see you after the show."

## EVA

"What if we lose him?" Eva asked Lora outside in the car.

"Here," Lora said, showing the tracking dot of Sam's dream catcher charm on her phone's app. "Jedi just set these up. With good satellite connection, it should accurately track to within a metre, anywhere on the globe."

Eva sighed. "Let's hope Jedi's technology is as good as he says it is."

*Don't get lost, Sam, we need you.*

## SAM

Listening to the second half of the show backstage, Sam occupied himself at the catering tables and tried to look relaxed, then killed time by leaning on a wall to watch some roadies playing pool. *Is this how an ultra-cool music journalist behaves?*

He listened to the encores and found his heart racing as he heard the band fall silent. He saw on an internal monitor that the house lights had come on.

*Gabriella will be here any second.*

"Hi," a voice said.

Sam turned around.

It was Gabriella.

*Wow.*

"*You're* from *Vertigo* magazine?" she asked, her English

coloured with her heavy Italian accent. She pointed to the press pass that hung around Sam's neck. She tilted her head quizzically, staring intently at Sam in a very unsettling way. "Sam. It's a cute name."

"Um. I guess so, yeah. Sam. I mean, I'm Sam. You're Gab—Gabriella."

"Well," Gabriella said, giving him a curious look. "If you want to interview me, Sam, you'll have to wait. I have to go get changed." She gestured to the stage costume she was still wearing, which could best be described as some kind of fairytale princess gown covered in tiny shimmering mirror fragments.

"Right," Sam said, stifling a dry cough. "Of course, no problem."

*Oh man, stop talking!*

"Or," she said, "you could just interview me at my party tonight?" She smiled a megawatt smile.

*Double wow.*

"OK, sure, thanks, great idea," Sam mumbled. He forced his lips together so no more embarrassing words could get out.

Gabriella began to walk away, then turned to say, "I'll meet you after I've finished my TV interviews. Wait here, *Sam.*"

"**S**am . . . can you talk? How's it going?" Lora whispered into his earpiece.

"Good. I think."

Eva said, "Have you met her?"

"Gabriella, yeah."

"And?"

"And? She's pretty."

Eva snorted a laugh. "Great, here we are trying to save the world from the forces of evil, and you're checking out pretty girls."

"Girl. Singular—there's just one of her."

"You're unbelievable!" Eva said.

"Sam, what's happening in there?" Lora asked, her voice full of calm reason.

"Sorry. Right, well, I've met her, and she wants me to interview her at the party," Sam said into his mic. He could feel his panic starting to rise. "That seemed too easy, don't you think?"

"Try not to worry too much. You dreamed about her, which means she's probably already had true dreams by now. She may have been expecting you."

"How do I know? I can't just open with 'Hey, did you dream about me last night?' Her security guards look tough, I could end up in serious trouble if I misjudge her. And she might freak out if she's already dreamed some of tonight. I thought I was going crazy when I met you in person after dreaming about you."

"Take a deep breath, slow down. It's alright to be apprehensive. But you *have* dreamed this, trust your intuition," Lora said.

"Thanks," Sam replied, then saw movement headed his way and panicked. "Going offline—here she comes."

"Hey, you," Gabriella said to him.

"Hey back," was all that Sam could manage. *Get a grip!*

"Coming with us?"

"Sure." He fell into step with her entourage as they walked down into the parking garage.

*I'm just getting in a car with Gabriella to go to her birthday party in Rome. Totally normal day.*

*Who am I kidding? This is so surreal.*

"There's nothing to worry about," Gabriella said to Sam as he clung on tight to the armrest. The driver of her limousine, trailing a car in front parting the light traffic, was weaving through the streets and speeding like a maniac. "My driver does this to lose the paparazzi."

"You sure we won't lose our lives in the process?" Sam asked, managing a nervous laugh as the driver flashed through an intersection at warp speed.

Gabriella looked at him and smiled. She leaned forward and asked her driver to slow down a little. "Better, yes?"

"Thanks." Sam glanced over his shoulder, and in the distance could just make out the car with Lora and Eva following them, along with the Guardians on their motorbikes. In this car, it was just the two of them in the back, her bodyguard riding in the passenger seat up front. "So, today's your birthday?"

"*Si*," she replied, "nice to know that the magazines get some things right."

"Well, happy birthday," Sam said, watching Rome strobe by outside the windows. "So, what's it like being a pop princess?"

She smiled but didn't laugh, and said, "It's bizarre. That's the right word, yes?"

"If you mean strange, then yes. Is your life strange?"

"Sometimes. Sometimes it's the best thing in the world. Other times it's the loneliest thing."

*Really? The party in my dream was off the hook! Her house is a palace, she's basically living the dream life.*

Sam continued, "What about your friends, your family?" He instantly regretted it when it almost looked like her eyes welled up with tears. But she smiled through it, well-practised at putting on her best face.

"Off the record?" she said.

Sam belatedly remembered his cover as a music reporter. "Sure, of course."

"All this? It adds up to exactly nothing," she said. "Becoming famous, I lost all my friends and I've been schooled alone since I was ten. Everyone around me works for me—they're *paid* to like me."

"But you know that it appears to so many on the outside, to your fans, that you're living the dream."

"Maybe, but it's not the truth," Gabriella looked at him, and her mood shifted a little. "Ha, look at me, talking 'off the record' to a stranger."

"I won't betray your trust," Sam said.

Gabriella smiled. "I know, I don't know why, but I know I can trust you, Sam."

"Ha, thanks," Sam laughed a weird, self-conscious laugh. *Get it together!* "OK, so what's your dream? If you could change how things are . . ."

"Sam, I have such crazy dreams, you don't believe it." There was a genuine smile that touched her eyes.

"Me too," Sam said. "Like *you* wouldn't believe . . ."

"Perhaps you should tell me about them."

"Maybe later," Sam said, a little unsure of how to ease into the saving-the-world subject now that the opportunity had finally presented itself.

Sam was just plucking up the courage to launch into his prepared speech when they pulled up outside Gabriella's palatial house in inner-city Rome. *Man, I should have told her already. I may not get another chance. Idiot!*

"Ah, about those dreams—" As they got out of the limousine, Sam could see that the party was well underway, and that Gabriella's concept of lonely might be far different to his. At least three hundred guests, mainly their own age, were milling about by the huge pool and immaculate gardens to welcome Gabriella as she exited the car. Dozens of cameras flashed and Sam did his best to remain out of shot.

"Come on!" Gabriella yelled, leading him up the stairs onto the paved area surrounding the pool.

"Who *are* all these people?" Sam yelled over pulsating music, as Gabriella shook hands and kissed cheeks as they pushed through the crowd, heading toward the house.

"Fans, people from my record labels, hangers-on who want their photos in magazines," Gabriella said loudly, not caring who might hear her. They reached the back patio and found a huge banquet table set up with at least a dozen waiters standing at attention. "Drink?"

"Water's fine."

She passed him a bottle of fancy Italian mineral

water and ushered him inside, pointing up a long marble staircase. "Up there, third door on the right."

Sam looked baffled. "What?"

"My bedroom."

He swallowed hard. "Say again?"

"Your *interview*," Gabriella said, with her beautiful Italian accent. "We'll get it over with first, then we can come downstairs, relax, and enjoy the party. Yes?"

"Ah, OK, third door on the right? Your bedroom."

"Yes. Relax, Sam. It's the only room that's off limits to all these people, so it'll be quiet. I'll see you there once I've said a few words."

"OK." Sam started up the imposing staircase, watching Gabriella ease effortlessly back into the throng of admirers.

*Oh, boy . . .*

"Um, so, I'm in her bedroom," Sam said into his phone.

"And what are you doing in there, Sam?" Eva said, surprised.

"I'm—anyway, what's happening out there? Any Agents?"

"Still nothing," Lora said. "But you have to act fast."

"No mucking around," Eva added.

"No mucking around intended," Sam said, his smile obvious, even over the phone.

"Right," Lora said. "Sam, just remember your dream and what hap—"

There was a noise at the door.

"Gotta go," Sam said, hanging up abruptly.

"Were you talking to someone?" Gabriella said as she entered the room.

"Just had to make a call."

"Right," Gabriella said. She gave him a measured stare, crossed her arms and stood near the door. "So, Sam. You'll never guess who I bumped into downstairs."

"The Pope?"

"Don't be cute."

Sam felt a lead weight in his stomach, knowing what she was going to say.

"The writer from *Vertigo* magazine," she said, eyeballing Sam carefully.

"Oh."

"Want me to bring her up here to clear things up?" she said, her hands on her hips.

"I don't think that's a good idea," Sam said.

"I see."

"Gabriella, please—"

"You've got two minutes," she said. "Who are you and what do you want?"

"So you're saying that my dreams are a kind of premonition that will lead us to some—what?"

"I'm not sure exactly. My dreams now seem to lead me to other Dreamers. I think you will have a dream about something that helps us in this race." Sam felt a little sick hearing himself say the words, trying to convince this girl. *Come on, think! She's not going to come on board with something so vague.*

"What race? To where?"

*Don't say "the ultimate battle of good against evil." She'll think you're some apocalyptic psycho and run for it.*

"I'm not completely sure of that either. There's a prophecy, and whether we like it or not, it has started a race—us against, well, some bad guys," Sam said. "They showed me the translation. All this stuff is pretty ancient but there have been things that I can't explain—"

"And wait, who's 'they'?" she asked.

"The Academy," Sam said.

"How many of 'us' are there?"

"Dreamers? Plenty. But the prophecy says that the last 13 will take on Solaris."

"That's one of the bad guys," Gabriella said.

"Yep." Sam tried what he hoped was a trustworthy smile.

"While being hunted by Enterprise Agents, the other bad guys you mentioned before," she added.

"Exactly."

"What do they want?"

"I'm not sure, but nothing good," Sam said.

"So, we have got *two* evil forces after us," Gabriella continued, "and you and I and the rest of the last 13 must find something—you're not sure what—before all these bad guys do. Otherwise?"

"Didn't I say?" Sam hedged.

"No, you didn't." Gabriella's eyes bored into Sam's.

"I thought this was the part where you made the connections . . ." Sam trailed off hopefully.

"What?"

"Right." Sam sat forward in his chair and cleared his throat. "Look, not to make it sound too much like Armageddon, but if we fail, the world will fall into an age of darkness."

Gabriella tilted her head. "Explain *darkness*."

"The world will—well, let's just say that everyone you care about will no longer have any control over their lives. It will be like a waking nightmare for everyone, forever."

"*Ma sei pazzo?*" she said. Sam looked blankly at her. "I

said, are you crazy?" she repeated, in English this time.

"Look, I know it's a lot to take in but you have to believe me." Sam turned his head to listen, unsure whether he'd heard a commotion outside.

"Because my life depends on it, *si*?"

"Well—"

"Am I the first person to follow my dream or something?" Sam detected her note of sarcasm.

"No, but it's different for us," Sam said. "Don't you feel that you've had a dream come true recently?"

"Look around you—as you say, I'm living the dream."

Sam was not put off by her tone this time.

"So, how about it? Ready for some adventure?" Sam felt as if time itself had stood still as the silence swirled around them. Gabriella's face was impossible to read. *What's she thinking?*

"OK." Gabriella stood. "I'm in."

"OK?" *Did I hear that right?*

"I believe you, Sam," she said.

"I know I shouldn't ask, but why?" he said.

She paused, weighing up her next words. "How about if I told you that your face seemed familiar when we met? I don't usually invite reporters to my bedroom, you know," she gave a short laugh. "But a few nights ago, I *did* have a dream—I don't remember much but you were there. I was running with you. We were looking for a book—an *old* book, in a dark place made of bookshelves, and we didn't have much time. Crazy, huh?"

"Not at all," Sam smiled. "It's all starting to make perfect sense, actually."

"So, what do we do now?" Gabriella said. "What's our next step in this adventure?"

"Well, we need to work out where we're going first," Sam said. He tried to look confident even though he didn't feel it. "Do you trust me?"

"Depends," she replied warily, as Sam pulled out the portable dream machine.

"I need you to put these on," Sam said, holding out the little tabs connected to the portable dream-reading machine, motioning for Gabriella to place them on her temples. She paused, her face full of doubt, before slowly following his instructions.

"It'll be fine, I promise. Now, we don't have a lot of time and the machine only works when . . . you have to think hard, about your dream, or, um, the things you saw, or . . ." Sam trailed off, aware he wasn't exactly sounding particularly inspiring or helpful.

He took his phone out of his pocket and dialled, trying to keep his hands steady and unaffected by the urgency.

"Lora, it's me. Gabriella has already had her dream. She's here now, hooked up to the machine. I just need some help running her through it."

"OK, put me on speakerphone," said Lora, pausing briefly as Sam switched over to speaker. "Gabriella, I'm Lora. I'm going to help you to recall the part of your dream that will help you and Sam. I know it feels a bit strange right now, but this is crucial—you must try to relax and really focus on what in your dream you think was important, OK?"

Gabriella nodded and looked from the phone to Sam, "I'll try."

"Can you remember what that might be?" Lora asked, her voice calm and reassuring.

"We were running, I think someone was chasing us. We found a book . . ."

"Good. That's good, Gabriella. Concentrate, but try not to force it," said Lora. "Clear your mind of everything around you, think of nothing else, except what you need to see . . ."

## GABRIELLA'S NIGHTMARE

At first, Gabriella was aware that she was in a dream. It was like she was watching herself from a distance, and she had the overwhelming déjà vu feeling of having done this and been here before. But that sensation quickly trickled away and she felt immersed in the dream's reality—as if she'd gone from snorkelling at the surface of the ocean and looking down at the fish to swimming among them.

There are people laughing and smiling as I walk by, rushing forward to greet me and wish me happy birthday. The party is a blur of noise and faces, and I move through the crowd until I spot the cute boy I've been talking to here. As I turn to him, it is as if his face is freeze-framed, like a photo. It's *him*. Sam.

He tells me a story, about a race, that we must act fast to beat the forces against us.

"What race? To where?" I say. The words echo in my head, didn't I just say that? *Concentrate, Gabriella . . . the book.*

He tells me about our amazing dreams. I believe this boy. I know what he is saying is true.

*Find the book.*

I ask him, "What book?"

He smiles at me, says, "It's your dream, you tell me."

I force my mind to picture it. *What did it look like?*

Time seems to pause, and then suddenly to skip . . .

There's yelling and shouting and people at the party are running everywhere.

We're running, too. Sam is next to me. He says to trust myself, to lead us where we need to go.

"Gabriella!"

I blink and see that we're now far, far away from the party. Sam is ahead of me, waiting.

"This way!" I call out to him to follow me in another direction.

We are in a maze.

We run through a corridor of tall bookshelves, the world around us dark and huge, as though we are in a massive subterranean chamber that stores every book in the world in the largest maze in the world. My heart beats wildly inside my chest as I realize that we are not running to find someone—we're running *from* someone.

They are chasing us, getting nearer. It's dark, the only light from dusty light globes swaying gently high above.

As we run, I catch my reflection and stop—there is a glass cabinet, a book locked inside. I don't hesitate, my hand seems to reach through the glass doors and I pick it up out of its cradle.

"What are you doing?" Sam says.

"We need this," I say.

"You're sure?" he says.

"Do you trust me?"

He hesitates for only a split second. "Yes! Now, go, run!"

Sam puts the book into his bag as I lead him down the aisles of shelves, row after row. A man appears out of nowhere, but somehow I know he is not our enemy. I look deep into his eyes and for a moment we share a connection, an understanding. He will help us.

We stumble through the maze of shelves, twisting and turning, running toward an unknown grotto. I know just where to go.

I lead us straight into a dead end. Sam looks at me, questioning.

The chase is closing in on us.

"This is it, I'm sure!" I say, but confusion is starting to surface, a panic is taking hold, and I'm finding it hard to breathe.

"The books—try the books!" I say, and we start to pull books from shelves.

"There are too many, we don't have time!"

"This one," I say, my voice calm, and I walk forward and pull on the spine of a blue book. There's a click and then the creaking of old, worn hinges moving a heavy door. The bookshelf opens to reveal a tunnel behind.

Behind us, footsteps draw near.

We look at each other, then run into the darkness together.

Where is the boy?

"Sam?"

No answer.

I don't see him but I'm carrying his bag. I feel the cold night air on my face and I realize I am wet, shivering. I spin around, trying to get my bearings. The cobbled streets are familiar. I'm still in Rome, but where? It must be late, there are only a few people walking past me, oblivious to my panicked heartbeat and dangerous situation. Should I be telling them to run? I know there are people chasing me. They can't be far behind. *Where is Sam?*

Someone bumps into me, I spin around but suddenly no one is there. The entire square is completely empty. Panic rises up to my throat, choking me.

*I am all alone.*

I turn back, but all I can see is a dark statue ahead.

Walking toward it, I pull out my phone, I must call my body-guards. But it's soaked, useless. Suddenly everything is deathly still. I look down at my hands. They are trembling, but it is not from the cold.

From the shadows beyond the fountain, I see someone.

"Sam!" I call out but no answer comes.

The dark figure moves toward me, seeming to float over the ground.

It is not Sam. It is an apparition. A seething dark mass, shaped like a tall man, moving toward me, everything about its appearance and intent, sinister.

I start to run away but I know in my heart there is no point. This thing will chase me down—it wants the book.

Over my shoulder I see him coming, faster and faster. In an impossible moment, he is right behind me, his breathing slow, mechanical and even as he reaches out a gloved hand. The sound of his metallic voice seems to come at me from all directions.

"Give me the book . . ." The voice rattles through my body, my bones aching with the sound.

"I won't!" I shout, but my shout turns to a cry of pain as he grips my arm. "You will not win! Only I can find it!"

I'm screaming, screaming, but no one hears me, no one comes.

I struggle with all that I have as I look into the black, lifeless mask of this demon. I close my eyes . . .

*I am all alone.*

## SAM

"It's OK, it's OK, I've got you," Sam whispered.

"What? Where am I?" Gabriella stammered. She looked up and was shocked to see she was still in her house. Her memory came back in a rush, "That machine—I was back in the dream I had days ago? It was a *nightmare*."

"You did well," Sam said, trying to soothe her nerves. Her face was flushed red and beaded with sweat. "It can be very unnerving to use the machine, but we learned a lot from it. You saw which book we need, right?"

"I did, and which library too," Gabriella said, before the reason for her panic came rushing back, "but there was a man! And we were trying to get away from him . . . and you—" she faltered. "I couldn't find you and then he was there, hurting me, and I was alone . . ."

"Sam, time to get moving," Lora's voice cautioned over the phone. "You guys are making great progress but you're outstaying your welcome."

Sam replied, "On our way."

"What does your friend say?" Gabriella smiled weakly,

the colour starting to return to her face as she tried to loosen the nightmare's grip.

"*Our* friend, Lora, says it's time to go," Sam said, pocketing his phone. He walked out onto the small balcony and peered over. Below on the patio stood a birthday cake, a model of the Tower of Pisa, almost two metres tall. Guests still milled about, laughing and dancing to the Europop music down below. It looked like a bigger drop than he'd seen in his dream.

*Well, I guess any paparazzi watching are about to get a photo that'll sell millions of magazines.*

"That's nearly a full-size replica," Sam said, pointing to the cake.

"I grew up in Pisa," Gabriella said, as she joined him on the balcony.

"We need to go," Sam said.

"Where to?" Gabriella said.

"Somewhere safe. Tell me, is that cake made of sponge?" Sam said.

"Yes, I think so. Why?"

"Ah, well . . ."

*Might be a softer landing than the one I dreamed.*

"Sam, we are safe here, I've got gates and cameras, and security."

"No," Sam said, shaking his head. "We have to leave in your red Ferrari."

"I don't have a Ferrari."

"Maserati?" Sam asked.

"I have a scooter," Gabriella offered.

Sam was stunned. "Maybe your dad has a car here?"

"No car, just the record company limo, but it's probably gone."

"Right," he said. "Scooter it is then."

"Now?"

"Did I not mention the part about the bad guys storming the room at any moment?" Sam said.

"And now I'm wondering why you didn't *start* with the part about the bad guys storming the room!" Gabriella complained.

Sam shrugged. "Sorry. Ready?"

"Can I pack a bag?"

Sam hesitated. *Pack a bag—is she serious?*

"No, sorry, we have to leave here right—"

*SMASH!*

"—now!"

Two massive guys burst into the room. Her security guards, right on cue.

"What is it?" she screamed at them.

"Security breach," the biggest guy said. "We have to get you to a safe—"

Before he could finish, he and his comrade slumped forward, several small darts spiked into their backs.

"We have to jump!" Sam said. He took Gabriella by the arm and they leapt as the Enterprise Agents stormed the room.

He could hear the startled cries of guests as they fell, landing squarely in the cake, sending it flying in all directions.

"They're here!" Sam shouted into his phone mic as he struggled to get out of the mass of iced sponge cake. He found Gabriella's wrist and looked around to get his bearings. Up at the balcony he saw the Agents trying to get a clear aim at them.

Gabriella fended off the helping hands of a dozen partygoers. Amid the confusion, people didn't know whether to call for help or give a round of applause.

"Hurry!" Sam said, dragging Gabriella to her feet and running under the cover of the terrace as the Enterprise Agents sent more darts fizzing through the air around them. The now-scattering guests shouted out in surprise and fear.

*THUMP! THUMP!*

Two darts smashed into the pavement right where they'd just been.

"We need to get outta here fast!"

"OK—follow me!" she yelled.

"Come on!" Gabriella said, going straight to her scooter as they ran into the dark garage.

The garage was in shadow but for a small spotlight on something big and covered in wrapping paper.

"Look!" Sam said, pointing to the present, which had the unmistakable shape of—

"A Maserati! No wonder I dreamed about driving," Gabriella said, running over to it and pulling off the bow-wrapped car cover to reveal the gleaming red sports car underneath. A small birthday card was tucked under a windshield wiper. "It's from my father! Oh, that's so sweet . . ."

*"You're reading the card?"* Sam said. "We have to move!"

Even though he was prepared, Sam's fingernails still dug into the dashboard of the sports car as Gabriella tore out of the garage and merged with the Rome traffic in a cloud of burning rubber.

"You have driven one of these before, right?" Sam asked.

"One of these?" Gabriella replied, flicking the steering wheel as she sent the car sliding sideways through the traffic and made a wide turn around the Colosseum. "I have never driven any car before!"

"Lora!" Sam said into his phone. He looked over his shoulder. "Yes, I see you—look out behind you!"

Behind Lora and Eva's car and the Guardians' motorbikes hard behind them, there were four blacked-out vehicles—the Enterprise. He saw Lora pull away hard to avoid an impact.

*Oh no!*

"Get down!" Sam yelled at Gabriella, the two of them sinking low in their seats as an Enterprise car bumped in hard behind them.

"Hey!" Gabriella cried out, looking over her shoulder with a furious expression.

"Watch the road!" Sam said, and they swerved to miss an oncoming taxi.

A loud noise and mess of glass exploded in the car—the rear-window had been shot out by their pursuers.

"I thought you said they used dart guns! Who are these guys?" Sam said into his phone. He couldn't make out the reply as he watched his friends' car careen fast across the road and ram against one of the Enterprise vehicles.

"*Yes!*" Sam yelled in momentary triumph.

Gabriella expertly down-shifted, swerved, and man-oeuvred to avoid a collision, still with three Enterprise cars hot on their tail.

Sam, impressed with the manoeuvre, said, "You've never driven?"

"I play racing games," Gabriella shrugged.

"I said they're shooting at the tires, trying to slow you down," Lora said, her voice sounding determined and calm over his earpiece.

"Well, they've got terrible aim!" Sam yelled.

"Where are you headed?" Lora replied.

"Hang on," Sam replied into the mic, then to Gabriella, "Do you know where you're going?"

Gabriella flew through the gears, the Maserati roaring, then she pulled the handbrake and they slid around a tight corner into a one-way street. Cars beeped and pulled out of the way as she threaded the needle.

"*Si*! Yes!" she said loudly over the toots and screams from the rest of Rome, her voice calm despite the vehicles still chasing them. "I know where that book is kept. The one we need. We are going there now!"

"**W**here is it?" Sam asked her, his stomach churning as the car went airborne over a rise in the road.

Gabriella wove through traffic like some kind of insane stunt driver. She hit the brakes and the car came to a shuddering halt before sliding up to the side of a tourist coach.

"Hold on!" she said, slamming the car into reverse.

*CRASH!*

They smashed against the Enterprise car behind, which was now totalled, its occupants trapped inside. Gabriella put the Maserati back in first gear and planted her foot, the burning rubber forming a smokescreen behind them.

She asked, "Are they still there?"

Sam felt carsick as he twisted in the seat to look for—

"Yes!" he said, the two remaining vehicles in the chase emerging through the carnage, the furthest one trying to run a couple of Guardians on motorbikes off the road as Lora and Eva continued to follow them.

Sam held onto the door handle tightly. "You really know where to go?"

Gabriella was silent for a moment as she navigated the late-night traffic chaos of Rome. *There's barely any room and everyone's still going at breakneck speed . . .*

"I wasn't sure you'd believe me, ha!" she said, taking another sharp turn that had him pinned against the door.

She flicked her wrist and they shot around a couple of buses driving slowly in the middle of the road. Behind them, the Enterprise car horns blared as they tried to get past the lumbering buses. Gabriella had bought them some time.

"That *I* wouldn't believe *you?*" Sam said.

She nodded, slowed the car and they squeezed past a traffic accident to much shouting and abuse from those standing in the road.

"But then the bad guys burst in, and as we started to run from them, I realized that maybe it's not too impossible," she said. "Maybe I am right."

"OK, so where is this book kept?" Sam asked.

"Somewhere safe," Gabriella replied, pulling into an underground parking.

*At least this seems different. That's something.*

"Where?" he asked again.

"Here."

"Hang back . . . we'll lose them, and contact you when we're out . . ." Sam said to Lora on the phone, but he lost reception as they went down another level of the parking garage. Then, as Gabriella pulled up and parked in a cloud of brake and tire dust, he saw the sign on the walls.

"No way . . ."

"*Si,*" Gabriella said, already out of the car and running toward the stairwell.

Sam caught up to her. "*The* Vatican?"

"Is there another?" she replied blithely.

They ran up the stairs and out into an ancient courtyard.

"As in *the* Pope?" Sam said, his mind reeling.

"There is only the one," Gabriella said.

They approached guards standing in front of a tall metal gate.

Sam swallowed hard. *How do we break into the Vatican?*

Gabriella moved forward to talk to the guards and they seemed lost in her charm.

Sam's phone beeped with a text message from Lora.

**Waiting around corner, tracking your location. Call if you need backup.**

They passed through gates that were familiar to Sam from his dream.

"How did you convince the guards to let us in?"

Gabriella smiled. "I can be persuasive."

The stacks of books stretched out before them in the dark, monumental space.

"This is the wing of the Vatican library that holds their rare and forbidden books," Gabriella said as they sped down a wrought-iron spiral staircase.

Sam tripped on the last step and fell flat on his face. *Don't remember this part from my dream.* He hastily got to his feet and brushed himself off.

"How did you even recognize this place?" Sam asked in wonder. *Who is this girl?*

"Being famous has its advantages," Gabriella smiled. Then, in response to Sam's puzzled face, she added, "So I like books! It's not a crime, no? Come on, this way," she said, pausing at a few junctions before deciding on a direction.

"Are you sure you know where you're going?" Sam asked.

"I dreamed it, didn't I? I think it's this way," she said. They passed down rows and rows of shelves, each looking the same. Gradually, her sense of direction was becoming muddled and they stopped. Endless shelves of books stretched out in every direction.

"It has to be here!" she shouted.

"Stay calm, we'll find it together," Sam whispered. He gently took her hand in his but she pulled away.

"We're close, I know it. We must keep looking," she said.

They kept running through the dark warren, as if trapped in a silent, book-lined maze. A growing feeling of frustration threatened to overtake Sam's clear head as he frantically searched for something familiar.

Gabriella skidded to a stop and Sam bumped into her.

"What are you doing?" Sam whispered.

"That's it!" she said. "The book I saw in my dream!"

Gabriella looked at a book in a display cabinet. Sam shone the flashlight of his phone onto it. He looked around

the case for locks or an access door—nothing.

"We'll have to break it. It's why we came here," Gabriella said as she smashed the glass with Sam's phone and lifted out the book within. It had thick yellowed pages and black leather binding, and the Roman numerals XII on the cover. "I had this book with me in the piazza . . ." Gabriella seemed lost as she struggled to replay her dream. "I'm sure I know it."

"Any place but here sounds good to me," Sam replied, putting the book in his backpack. "Let's go."

They ran around the next corner—

"Argh!" Sam screamed.

The man in black from their dreams stood before them. This time Sam noticed the little white square at the front of his collar—*he's a priest!*

Gabriella said something apologetic to him as he protested, telling them off in Italian. But then Gabriella talked to him again, her tone soothing and calm, and he slowly nodded and replied, pointing down the corridor of bookcases from where he'd come.

"What on earth did you *say?*" Sam whispered, smiling at the priest in what he hoped was a winning way.

"I told him to trust me," she said. "That us being here is destiny."

"Wow. And what did *he* say?" Sam asked.

"To take the next two rights, go all the way to the end and turn left, and there we'll find a secret doorway that leads to a grotto," Gabriella said. "And that he will try to delay them."

Sam said, "Them?"

They heard the sound of many feet, running their way. *The Agents . . .*

The priest disappeared around a corner, quickly followed by crashing noises as shelves of books were tipped over.

Sam began to run, but then Gabriella stopped in front of him at the first right. The way ahead was in near darkness.

Sam pulled her onward, and they came to the second right-hand turn, fumbling their way onward in the gloom—

*THWACK!*

A dart hit the tall wood bookcase right where his head had just been. Sam tugged at the nearest bookcase to bring it down, but it wouldn't budge. He heaved and shoved, and Gabriella helped, and they just began to get it moving when—

*WRANG!*

A net wrapped around the shelf just as it started to tumble, long steel spikes snapping it taut by biting into the wood and books.

Sam was stuck, his right arm trapped under the net.

"Go!" Sam said, crouching on the floor, struggling to free his arm from the tight net strings. He could see them now, four Enterprise Agents, running toward them.

Gabriella pulled at his other arm. "Not without you!"

"*Go!*"

"No!"

The lead Agent pulled up a weapon to fire—

*PFFT!*

Time seemed to slow for Sam, as he tore free from the net—his jacket sleeve remaining behind—and he wriggled behind the fallen bookcase, following Gabriella into the darkness beyond.

They stood at the dead end wall of books.

"The book spines—we must find the secret doorway!" Gabriella whispered.

Sam watched as she frantically pulled at several books then quickly followed suit.

"I can't remember the title!" she said, panicking.

They could hear the commotion of Agents running in the maze of book stacks, closer every second.

"Slow down, try to visualize it from your dream, what colour did you see?" he said.

"It—was blue!" she said with sudden clarity. "The spine was blue!"

"Dozens of them are blue," Sam said, grabbing at spines.

"It was at eye level," she said, "somewhere around here—"

*CRACK!*

The book under her fingers tipped outward and released

a latch. The sound of hinges creaking echoed as a door started to open.

*WHACK!*

A dart thumped into Sam's backpack. Without a word he grabbed Gabriella.

The wall-sized bookcase with its hundreds of books opened just enough, and amid the overwhelming noise and dust and commotion, they disappeared behind it.

Their footsteps echoed loudly as they sprinted down the dusty, fetid corridor, both of them wincing at each loud stomp they made, the way ahead lit only by the light on Sam's phone. Cobwebs tangled in their hair as they ran down a smooth cobbled ramp. They skidded to a stop as they came out into a damp, dark cavern but the momentum was carrying them too fast. They fell feet first into the swirling lake below. The water was so cold that Gabriella shrieked as she broke the surface. Sam gasped and coughed in the icy water, pulling her to the nearest of three gondolas that bobbed gently at the stone pier beside them.

"We don't have long," Sam said, dragging himself aboard after her. "Come on!"

Sam pushed off—

The lights of the Agents' flashlights could be seen in the tunnel behind them.

Sam heaved with the long oar, pushing them off. It was agonizingly slow to get moving.

"Paddle with your hands!" he told Gabriella, and she sat up the front and started to pull her shaking hands through the cold water.

There were noises back at the pier. Without warning, the sprinting figure of an Agent launched off the sandstone pier, arms outstretched toward them. He splashed into the water behind, *just* missing landing in the gondola, but with his hands holding tightly to the back of the boat.

Sam pulled the oar from the water and used it to prise the Agent off the wooden edge of the boat.

*WHACK!*

A dart embedded into the oar, right between Sam's eyes.

"Get down!" Sam yelled to Gabriella, tossing the oar into the gondola and diving down. The two of them reached over the sides and paddled as fast as they could, while the Agent in the water was swimming hard to catch up, trying again to climb into their boat.

This time Gabriella forced him off with a couple of swift kicks.

Sam paddled as fast as he could, an arm scooping each side of the gondola, the tunnel ahead nearing. He looked over his shoulder.

An Agent raised his reloaded net gun—

*WHOOSH!*

The Agent in the water pulled himself back onto the

boat just as the net hit and wrapped around him, yanking him back into the dark water and tearing off a chunk of the gondola's wood siding.

"Quick!" Gabriella cried. "Now's our chance to get away!"

Sam threw his weight into leveraging the oar, their momentum in the water now fast enough for it to be useful to keep propelling them.

They approached the tunnel entrances—there were two to choose from. They had gone right in his dream . . .

"Gabriella, which tunnel?"

"The priest told me to go right. It's the fastest way out."

Sam looked at her apprehensively. Solaris flashed through his mind. *He's not here so maybe we've already outrun the dream? But still . . .*

"So, left then?"

She nodded and they entered the left tunnel. *So far so—*

Noises behind.

The Agent reloaded his net-gun.

"Down!"

*SPLASH!*

A net landed violently in the water behind them, the gondola tilting wildly in its wake. Sam pushed on. They were farther into the tunnel this time, compared to his dream. *Maybe we're in the clear . . .*

*WHACK! WHACK! WHACK!*

Darts bored into the gondola, splinters of wood flying through the air.

Gabriella screamed.

Sam pushed as hard and fast as he could with the oar, as he saw Agents boarding a gondola, and then—

*WHOOSH! WHACK!*

Another fast-flying net, this time hitting the top of the tunnel, taking out a cracked support beam in the ceiling. Sam pushed frantically into the black water with the oar, trying desperately to increase the speed of the antiquated vessel. Gabriella was looking directly at Sam, her eyes wide with fear. Overhead he could hear the ominous rumbling and tumbling of the stones as the tunnel collapsed around them.

**G**abriella's scream took a while to die down.

"We're safe," Sam said, calming her down by sitting with her in the gondola and holding her hands, her frightened face illuminated by his little phone light. "It's OK now. Wow, you sure have some pipes on you."

"Pipes?" Gabriella said.

"Vocal pipes, your voice. You're very loud, when you want to be."

She gave Sam a nervous smile.

Sam shone the phone's light back down the tunnel for one last look at the entrance that had nearly buried them in rocks—it was completely impassable, tons of stone and rubble blocking it off. *No way the Agents will get through that in a hurry.*

"Well, I guess we now get to see where this tunnel leads," Sam said, and passed Gabriella his phone as he pushed off with the oar. He smiled, elated at having outrun his fate. But his smile faded as he thought of what might lie ahead.

The tunnel ended at a small stone platform. A rusted steel door was inset into the wall, held shut by a bar set across it.

Sam helped Gabriella out of the gondola and they tried lifting the bar from the door. It creaked and moaned and eventually popped free and clattered to the ground with an almighty *CLANG!*

The door opened toward them, slowly, bit by bit, against aged, rusty hinges.

Beyond was a room the size of a broom closet. Peering harder into the darkness Sam could faintly make out metal rungs set into the wall, disappearing into the void above. *A way out.*

"Looks like we gotta climb."

Gabriella hesitated and pulled at Sam's sleeve. "But my dream . . . the man in black was above, waiting for me. I don't think I can . . ." her eyes welled up with fearful tears.

"It's OK, I'm here now," Sam said gently. "We're not even coming out in the same place. We changed it."

Gabriella looked unconvinced. "Don't leave me, Sam. I don't want to be alone."

Sam gave her a brief hug and smiled. "We'll have back-up, don't worry."

At the top of the ladder the square manhole cover seemed to weigh about as much as the bookcase in the Vatican. After a few minutes of pushing and shoving, Sam managed to lift it just enough to slide the door's bar through, then he used that as a lever, heaved the cover up and pushed it across the ground with an ear-splitting grating noise.

He climbed out and fell into a heap on a smooth cobblestone surface, a starry sky above them.

"This isn't the place from my dream," Gabriella said, her eyes darting around the quiet piazza as Sam helped her out of the manhole. He could hear the fear in Gabriella's voice. "The Campo de' Fiori!" Gabriella said, her eyes wide with recognition. "We're in Campo de' Fiori!"

"Stay calm," said Sam, looking around the empty civic square and catching his breath.

"But couldn't he still find us? He's looking for me—and that book," Gabriella shot back. "Sam, I want to go. Now."

"No problem, follow me," Sam said, recognizing she was going into shock. He pointed toward a narrow alley branching off from the square. "We'll head down that way, out of the open, and I'll call for us to get picked up."

Sam and Gabriella waited in an old sandstone doorway while he called Lora, silently thanking Jedi for making his phone, and bag, waterproof.

Sam was starting to feel more confident in his task now that he had survived his fatal premonition. He looked at Gabriella pressed hard against the wooden door behind her, obviously still anxious and afraid, and trying to conceal as much of herself as possible in the shadows.

"So, who was that statue of, back there in the square?"

"Giordano Bruno," Gabriella said.

"He was holding a book too," said Sam. *Huh*.

"Time to find out what we've got," Sam said, taking off his backpack and pulling out the heavy old book. "There's this XII marking on the outside and a clasp at the side, looks old . . ."

They both studied the book resting on Sam's knees, just able to make out the details in the alley streetlight.

"Strange . . . this book has no title, no other markings," Gabriella murmured.

"Maybe it's not a book," Sam said, studying the shoebox-sized book from all angles. "It feels way heavier than it should."

"And, it's locked." Gabriella pointed to the brass clasp holding the cover shut.

Sam looked closer at the clasp on the side, set with a tiny keyhole.

*A star-shaped lock!*

Sam took off his dream catcher necklace and produced the golden key. He inserted it into the locking mechanism, turning it gently.

"Stop!" Gabriella said.

Sam looked at her, her expression still anxious.

"What if we're not supposed to open it? I mean, I *feel* that we are, but what if it could release something evil?"

"Well, I don't know for sure what will happen, but we have to trust our instincts," Sam said, repeating the

Professor's advice. "We must have dreamed all these things for a reason, don't you think? Besides, I don't think an old book is going to give us any problems."

Gabriella nodded and bit her lip.

"OK, here goes . . ."

He turned the key.

*CLICK*.

## ALEX

From his vantage point outside the door of the operations room, Alex could hear the voices clearly. He squinted through the narrow gap in the door, and could see the Director standing at the end of a long boardroom table. One entire wall was covered with images of Sam taken in New York.

Phoebe was sitting at the table. When she had been paged earlier to attend this urgent meeting, she had told Alex to look around the facilities—this seemed as good a place as any to start.

"We lost him," Stella said, her image on a big screen on the wall. "He got away from us underneath the Vatican."

"Blasted!" Jack replied, pounding his powerful prosthetic fist down on the table, the impact making a loud metallic sound.

"Who was the next Dreamer?" he asked.

"Uploading now," an operator answered.

Alex recognized the image immediately. It was of the Italian pop star, Gabriella. Her details came up on screen.

"OK . . ."

Alex shifted his position slightly so he could see farther into the room.

The Director spoke again, aiming his fury at everyone. "So this time it's not one of ours, but that might just be a fluke. We're going to have to make sure all the surrogate parents are on high alert. We can't have this happen again."

Stella replied, "There are over a thousand kids that age, all over the world. We don't know if any of them might be part of the last 13 until they are—"

"I am fully aware of the process, Agent Wilde. I want you to stay out there, keep mobile, keep looking and put together rapid-response teams on each continent," the Director ordered. "Dreamers cannot keep slipping through our fingers like this."

Internet news headlines flashed on a screen.

**LATEST HEADLINES //**

**VIOLENCE ERUPTS IN ROME**

Erica Leong

Police and security forces remain baffled at the sudden outbreak of violence that occurred in the city streets just moments ago. Authorities believe the attacks are somehow targeted and may possibly be related to rival gangs of some nature. The head of said, 'We urge Roman citi contain the situation.

**>> BREAKING NEWS <<**
**ROME IN CHAOS**

**STREETS TURNED INTO BATTLEGROUND**

Michael Webb

Dozens of people have been injured as unknown assailants seemingly wage war across the city of Rome. Reports from the capital indicate that authorities were completely unprepared for the chaos as armed gunmen careened through city streets, injuring passers-by during their rampage.

Stella paused. "And there's the other complication to consider."

"Solaris?" Jack asked.

Stella nodded.

"Where is he now?"

"I'm not sure. But I am certain he'll be here."

Alex pulled away from the door. Everyone was looking for Sam, including Solaris. Sam was in danger. *Maybe I can persuade him to join us at the Enterprise. They'd be far better at keeping him safe than the Academy. But then it's all about him again, isn't it?*

Alex leapt up and sprinted down the corridor as he heard footsteps approaching the door, his thoughts of Sam scattering as he ran.

Alex was in a computer lab. All the lights were off but for one lamp. He was reading up on the database of well-known Dreamers . . .

"Am I one of these people?" Alex wondered aloud.

"I'm not sure," a voice replied.

"Phoebe?" Alex turned, surprised to see his mother standing in the doorway.

"You can still call me Mom, you know," she chided. She came over and sat next to him.

"Right." Alex sighed.

"I know this is hard," she went on.

"It is what it is," he replied, looking at the screen in front of him. "Bits of it are even kind of cool."

Phoebe smiled. "What you up to?"

"Not much," Alex replied. "Meeting went well?"

"Mmm . . . there's so much work to do," she said.

Alex nodded. "Will you find Sam and Eva?"

"We're trying."

"And when you find them?"

Phoebe looked a little uncomfortable.

"I saw the headlines—whatever it was that happened in Rome. You were chasing Sam, right?" Alex said.

"Yes, that was us. But that's why the Academy should let us take charge in this race," Phoebe said. "It's too important to throw it all away on a petty rivalry and now you can see what happens when the situation isn't controlled. Innocent people get hurt."

Alex shook his head. There was so much to think about, his head ached.

"Look, I—we, Jack and the Enterprise—are trying to do something important for the world," Phoebe went on. "To take the innate abilities of Dreamers and use science and technology to make the most of those talents. We have trained Dreamers in high-ranking positions all over the world, who achieve all kinds of amazing things—saving lives, creating ground-breaking technologies, shaping the future." She sighed and took Alex's hand in her own.

"I hope I brought you up to think for yourself and to take control of your own life. I believe in those things and the Enterprise does too."

"So, you think I should stay here?" Alex asked.

"Yes, I do, but it's up to you. I know you'll make the right decision." Phoebe embraced him warmly.

The doors hissed open and the Director strode in. "Ah, I'm glad I've found you both. Have you discussed the matter with him yet, Phoebe?" he asked.

"No, we hadn't got around to that," Phoebe replied.

Alex looked from Jack to his mother. "What matter?"

# 30

**SAM**

"**O**K, so it's not a book," Sam whispered.

"What is it?" Gabriella asked, her eyes still closed.

"A box," Sam said, taking out a rolled piece of creased parchment and a little leather-bound journal. "With a smaller book and a map inside."

"Map? What map?" asked Gabriella, her eyes springing open.

"Not sure . . ." Sam replied absently. He was studying the book carefully, angling it as best he could to catch the light as he untied the strap around it.

"We'll have to get this back to the Academy, get the Professor and Jedi to look at it," Sam said as he gently leafed through the pages.

Gabriella reached over and took the map from Sam, unrolling the parchment and looking at the diagram while he flipped through the pages of the journal.

"Um, Sam," she said, pulling at his sleeve, "Sam, this map . . ."

"You know, it looks like this journal is written—"

"Sam! Maybe it is not the book we need, perhaps it is the map." Gabriella looked at it closely. "I remember now, *this* was in my dream also. The one I had a couple of nights ago when I saw you. This is the map that will lead us to what you need."

"Sounds good," Sam said, and looked around, wary. "We've been here long enough. Let's move—"

Sam stopped cold at the faint sound of footsteps echoing over the cobblestones.

"Sam?" Gabriella's voice wavered.

*THWACK! THWACK!*

Two stun darts landed in the peeling paint of the wooden door, close to Gabriella's arm.

"*Go!*" Sam screamed, pulling Gabriella up with him and running back into the piazza. Sam could make out three Agents on foot at the other end of the alley behind him.

At the corner of the square a car was pulling up with Lora and Eva practically hanging out the doors. From the left, Guardians roared in on motorbikes as two vans screeched into the square at full speed. A battle with the pursuing Agents erupted behind them as Sam and Gabriella sprinted toward the car. They jumped in the open side door when the car slowed for a moment and collapsed onto the backseat as it sped away from the battle.

"Eva, Lora, this is Gabriella," Sam gasped as the car lurched sideways around a corner.

They could only nod to each other as the high speed forced them to brace against the car doors.

The squeal of tires and accelerating engines could still be heard behind them. The faces of concerned onlookers at windows, woken by the sudden noise, flashed by as they flew through the winding streets.

"Are they gone?" Eva asked, looking out the rear window.

"Not for long," Lora replied, then spoke to the lead Guardian. "We'll head back to the Academy, but we need to lose this tail first."

"No," Sam said, showing the map to Lora, "change of plan. We need to decipher this and go there."

"Right. OK." Lora could see by the look on Sam's face that this was not the time to be asking questions.

For the second time that night Sam heard an ear-piercing crack followed by the shattering of glass, as the back window of the Academy car broke, pieces flying in a million different directions.

"Get down!"

*Yep, definitely not just darts anymore.*

The driver manoeuvred their speeding vehicle through narrow lanes and into the melee of Rome traffic. Sam held onto Gabriella as they were thrown around the back seat of the car. Although it was late, the main thoroughfares were still busy with the cars and buses of tourists and late-night revellers. Peering over the edge of their seats, Sam could see two Enterprise cars hot on their heels. Shouts of disapproval from bystanders occasionally rang out over the noise of the engine.

Their car continued to swerve wildly through backstreets and alleys, trying to lose their unwanted company.

Sam turned to Gabriella. "You know where we have to go now?"

"I don't, I can't remember!" she cried.

"Concentrate, your dream took you there," Sam said. "Think back, look for a clue that will help us read the map."

Gabriella closed her eyes, trying hard to concentrate as she was buffeted around the careening car. A minute later, she started to smile.

## 31

"This," Gabriella said, standing outside the car and looking up at the building, "is the Pantheon."

Sam wasn't quite sure what he was expecting, but it was bigger than he thought an ancient temple in the middle of a city would be. The huge concrete columns at the front of the building loomed over the four of them as they quickly walked across the piazza. A light rain began to fall, the stone ground slippery underfoot. They sheltered under the impressive portico.

They had managed to evade the remaining Agents in a wild car chase through Rome, weaving and wending in and out of laneways and dark streets, ending up close to where they had started. Now, all about them was eerie quiet, as if they were in the eye of the storm.

"Inside—what we need is inside," Gabriella said.

Sam walked over and tried pushing against the gigantic bronze doors. Locked. *Worth a try.*

Then he stopped. The rain too had stopped.

"What is it?" Eva said to him, an alarmed look in her eyes.

"It's like my dream in New York," Sam said. "Lora, does this suddenly feel weird to you? Got the déjà vu?"

Lora shook her head but her hand reached under her jacket for her dart gun. "We should—"

Across the piazza, a tall figure stood on the edge of darkness, watching them.

"RUN!" Lora shouted without hesitation, already pushing Sam toward the others.

The figure stepped out from the shadows, and for Sam, there was no doubting it this time. Dread washed over him like a tidal wave as the figure drew himself up to his full height and spread out his arms.

Solaris. *Now he's real.*

Lora raised her gun—

*FLASH!*

The fire streaming from Solaris' outstretched hand lit up the night as the fire-bolt roared across the distance between them. Lora instantly dropped her weapon as the heat seared the metal in her right hand, her glove smouldering dangerously as she frantically pulled it off. Solaris strode menacingly toward them and raised his palm again.

The Guardian in their car began firing as he took cover behind the vehicle, momentarily capturing Solaris' attention.

Sam instinctively reached out and pulled them all behind one of the massive columns of the Pantheon—just in time, as Solaris threw another jet of fire in their direction. He could feel the concrete pillar glowing red-hot from the burst of flames.

"We need a plan!" Sam yelled as they ran from the square.

They ran through the cobbled streets at full pelt, throwing backward glances as they went. But the maze of Roman streets hid them from Solaris' view as they scrambled through narrow lanes, turning and turning again to lose their pursuer.

They pulled up in a darkened alley and all was quiet again. But Lora was taking no risks. She found a small window that had been left open and led them through it into the tiny galley kitchen of a restaurant, already closed up for the night. The smell of disinfectant drifted up from the recently mopped floorboards as they caught their breath.

"He's . . . real . . ." Eva began, as her breathing finally slowed. Gabriella looked at her in silent shock, the horror of her nightmare coming true dawning on her.

"So about this plan," Sam started to say, but words failed him. Somehow he'd kept hoping that Solaris would turn out to be just a Dreamer bogeyman, not actual flesh and blood.

Lora looked pale. She said to Sam, "I know it's difficult,"

then paused before going on, "but we have to stay focused on Gabriella's dream—and what we have to do." She dialled the security team, wincing at the pain in her right hand.

Eva and Gabriella began rummaging through the drawers and cupboards of the kitchen, looking for something they could use to treat Lora's burn.

"The others are coming but they're at the edge of the city," Lora said, pocketing the phone. "Ten minutes."

"Do we stay here?" Sam asked.

"No, we're not safe," Lora said, moving away from the back door. "We have to keep moving, and be ready to make for the Pantheon when—"

*WHOMP!*

It was the unmistakable sound of Solaris' fire-bolt. Through the small window in the back door, they could see flames erupting against the darkness.

Sam's heart beat faster at the sight of the blaze, the flames licking higher and higher up the door.

"Run!" Lora yelled. "Out the front! *Run!*"

Sam was the last out the front door of the deserted restaurant, following the others through the obstacle course of neatly set tables and empty chairs.

*WHOMP!*

The door frame next to his head splintered and caught fire—

*WHOMP!*

Sam ducked and tumbled onto the street as a shot

melted a fist-sized hole clear through the glass door.

"Follow me!" Gabriella screamed. The three of them ran fast behind her, around the corner and into a late-night music venue, the ushers happily waving Gabriella and her friends in.

"I played here once," she explained, running through the busy club.

Hundreds of people were dancing and enjoying the party, blissfully unaware of what was taking place around them.

"Come," Gabriella said, "out the back!"

"It's too busy! All these people, we can't endanger them!" Lora said in protest.

A few seconds later shouts started to cascade through the throng of people.

"Solaris!" Sam said.

"No," Gabriella said. They were nearly through the crowd when her presence was noticed. "It's because of me."

"Move!" Lora said, the four of them forming a tight huddle as they pushed through the crowd, some of whom were reaching out to touch Gabriella.

There was another crescendo of screams, this time from the direction of the entrance, where they'd been a moment ago.

"*That's* Solaris," Sam said, his voice full of regret. *We shouldn't have come here.*

## ALEX

"You want me to work for you?" Alex asked. He was sitting with Jack and Phoebe on a bench within the manicured gardens surrounding the entrance to the impressive Enterprise building. Alex watched the evening tide of commuters dispersing from the neighbouring buildings.

"Not for us, but *with* us," his mother said. She put an arm around him. Alex continued to stare at all these people going about their normal lives, oblivious to the brewing danger for the time being.

"Sam's not the only one who can save the world," Jack said. "You can too, you're a vital part of this."

Alex looked to his mom.

"He's right," she said.

"And what does that mean—that I'm one of the last 13?"

"I believe it's possible, and that you can do anything he can," Jack said. "With our training, you can do it all and more."

"More?" Alex asked.

The Director laughed. "The Professor and his team don't encourage growth like we do. Like I said before, we like to accelerate things to make the most of your potential."

*I like the sound of that.*

"And I'd do what, exactly?" Alex asked carefully.

"You'd be participating directly in the race, for a start. Helping us to discover that ultimate power for humanity, for the world."

"But I'd do it with you, not the Academy?"

"It's all the same cause," his mother said. "We all want the same thing—to beat Solaris."

"We have to," Jack added.

Alex said, "Then why does the Academy disagree with you so much?"

"Because they're doing things their own way, following old outdated methods," Jack said. "And people fear what they don't understand."

Alex shook his head. He stood and walked over the soft grass.

"Everything we know as normal life will be over if we don't win the race," Phoebe said.

"I know."

"We need your help, your gift . . ." she trailed off.

Alex saw a mother walk by with her young son. *That could have been us ten years ago.*

"OK," he said, turning to them both. "OK, I'm in. When do I start?"

Alex understood the Enterprise was an efficient organization, but even he was surprised to find himself on his way to immediately begin his first assignment. As he walked with Phoebe and the Director back into the vast atrium and into one of the express glass elevators, Alex couldn't help but feel invigorated for the first time in days. He liked it here, and his instinct told him he would like whatever it was Jack had planned for him.

"And so we arrive at perhaps the most important area of our headquarters," the Director was saying as he led them down a stark corridor. In contrast to most of the other areas Alex had seen so far in this endless building, these halls were largely devoid of workers.

The Director held his hand, open-palmed, up to a square black scanner mounted on the wall beside the double doors at the end of the corridor. The doors hissed open, and he indicated for Phoebe and Alex to walk through, following them as they did.

"Welcome to our IT laboratory," Jack said, a hint of pride in his voice.

"Also known as Matrix's lair," Phoebe added with a chuckle.

It took a moment for Alex's eyes to adjust to the dim light. He looked around. Never before had he seen so many screens and hard drives, cables and machines all in one place. The room felt like a mammoth cavern, dark apart from the twinkling activity of data flowing over the screens. It was unnervingly quiet, only the faint hum of the computers, or the occasional cough of an Enterprise employee. In fact, it took a few minutes for Alex to even register that there were actually other people in the room—silent techies blending perfectly into their dark, high-tech habitat.

"Ah, here he is," said the Director looking to a man sitting over on the right in front of a large screen. "Matrix, this is Alex. I assume you received my memo about his role in your team."

Matrix continued to tap away at his keyboard for a moment, eventually turning in his chair to look at the trio beside him. His ragged stubble, long ponytail and the T-shirt he wore over his large stomach were in stark contrast to the neat technicians around him. "Yep, got it," he said, turning back to his keyboard.

"Good. Great," the Director said, clearly accustomed to Matrix's concise conversation style. "Well, I trust you'll action all the points in the memo. We'll leave Alex here in your capable hands." The Director turned to Alex. "Matrix is probably the most gifted technical mind on the planet. He will see that you are set up and given security clearance in order to work for him. Phoebe tells me you are a natural with computers, so I'm sure you'll be a great help to us."

The Director turned and left the room, with Phoebe sneaking Alex a quick smile and a thumbs-up before following him out.

Alex remained where he was, hands in his pockets, rocking on his heels. He was keen to get stuck in, all he needed was for Matrix to turn back around and notice him. *Clearly he's not in much of a hurry to save the world, then.*

Alex said, "So, can I do some—"

"Don't touch anything in here," Matrix said, without turning from his computer.

The door hissed open behind him. A tall guy wearing a buttoned-up shirt came in.

"Better yet," Matrix said over his shoulder, "this is your supervisor. Do everything he says."

"OK," Alex said, and outstretched a hand to the new arrival. "I'm Alex."

The guy smiled and shook Alex's hand. "I'm Shiva," he said.

## SAM

They doubled back through the streets until Gabriella led them toward the Pantheon once more. Crouched down on the other side of the wide piazza, they hid in the shadows of the old buildings. The silence around them made their ears feel numb after the throbbing noise of the nightclub. They waited, concealed in patches of darkness, hoping to go unnoticed both by security and Solaris.

"No sign of him," Eva said.

"He won't be far away," Lora said. "Is there another way in?"

"At the back," Gabriella pointed, "behind the rotunda."

"And you're sure that the map points to the Pantheon?" Lora asked.

"Yes—now, I'm sure," Gabriella replied. "I saw the altar in my dream."

"Says here that the altar was designed by Alessandro Specchi, in the 1700s," Sam said, consulting his phone, "and it's at the other end of the grand rotunda, directly opposite the front entr—"

"Move and talk," Lora said, then spoke into her phone to the Guardians.

"There they are!" Sam said, pointing in front of them.

Two black vans came to a screeching halt across the piazza. Six Guardians poured out, doing a sweep with their weapons. Lora ran toward them, still talking into the phone, and the armed men set up defensive positions as the others followed Lora across the piazza.

*WHOMP—WHOMP—WHOMP!*

Three bolts of super-hot flame hit the radiator grill of the lead vehicle. Sam watched it happen as though in slow motion.

The Guardians spilled out and ran for cover just as the vehicle exploded into a bright orange fireball and launched high into the air. A second explosion mid-air sent bits of metal flying everywhere.

Sam leapt up to shield Eva and Gabriella from the debris, but was hit square in the back by a large piece of the van's frame, knocking him flat.

"Sam, are you OK?" Eva asked.

"Yeah," he got to his feet, his legs wobbly underneath him.

"Wow!" Gabriella said.

Sam could see that parts of his back were smouldering with fire—and he pulled a large chunk of scorched steel from his shoulder. It hadn't cut him at all. The Stealth Suit had worked as an armoured suit and had protected him from the fire and debris.

"*Now* I'm really loving my Stealth Suit," Sam said, glad that something was finally going his way. In the piazza, he could make out the flaming wreckage of the Guardians' vehicle nearby. Terrified faces peered out from the rows of windows overlooking the square. Solaris was out of sight but Sam could guess his position by the streaming bolts of flame radiating out from the opposite corner of the square. The Guardians kept firing in that direction to keep him back.

Lora yelled back at Sam, "Get down and follow me!"

They ran fast toward the front of the Pantheon, ducking behind one of the eight towering granite columns of the temple's portico.

Despite the Guardians' staunch defence, Solaris was slowly approaching across the paved expanse, shooting a continuous stream of fire. The laser-like beam blasted through the base of the three-storey high stone pinnacle in the piazza's fountain.

*CRAAACK!*

The tall tower moaned as its base started to give way under the barrage of Solaris' fire. Sam saw movement at the top.

"It's coming down!" he yelled. They scrambled down the steps, away from the portico that was directly in its path—

"Eva!" Sam screamed over his shoulder. Eva remained

where she was, still clinging tightly to the concrete pillar, rooted to the spot in fear.

The fountain's obelisk was now leaning at a forty-five degree angle toward where Eva still stood. Then—

*SMASH!*

It gave in to the force of gravity and fell fast to the ground. Eva looked on in terror. She snapped out of her frozen panic and jumped back just in time. The stone rumbled in a heap across the piazza, the top of the fountain's column landing at Eva's feet.

"Stay there!" Sam yelled at her. "Stay with Lora—we'll meet you at the other side of the Pantheon!"

Sam and Gabriella ran down the north-west side of the Pantheon, skirting the outside of the rotunda. Gabriella pointed, "Here!" and showed Sam a set of rocky stairs at the back of the building. They could see a few late-night tourists craning their necks around the corner, curious about the mayhem that could be heard out front. Sam frantically waved them away, silently urging them to flee while they could.

The back entrance was devoid of any security, all drawn to the commotion playing out in the square. They heaved the green, aged brass door open.

Inside, the Pantheon was serenely quiet. As they crept

down the corridor through the chapel and entered the main temple, Sam couldn't help but stop and look around in awe. They were at one end of a vast hall, easily big enough to host a football game in. Above him a massive domed roof stretched high into the air, intricately decorated and with an open circular skylight at its apex. All around the walls under the dome, back-lit statues of gods, philosophers and religious figures looked on.

"It's incredible," Sam said, turning on the spot. Through the hole in the dome he could make out the stars and a small sliver of the moon.

"We're here!" Gabriella's voice was sharp and dragged Sam back to his urgent reality. "That's the altar."

Sam realized they were standing on the inside of a roped-off altar within a grand arched alcove. A row of tall ceremonial candles, each at least as tall as him, stood upright in huge golden stands.

"So now what?" Sam asked, his voice carrying around the void. "This building has been here for nearly two thousand years—what could there be to find that hasn't been discovered?"

"We have to look closer," Gabriella said. She walked over the intricately detailed marble floor, then up the stairs leading to the platform of the pulpit, Sam close behind.

"OK . . ." he said, looking around. There was a worn carpet on the floor and simple decorations around the inside of the altar. "Nothing. Maybe this wasn't—"

"I dreamed this . . ." Gabriella said, looking absently, her voice at a whisper yet carrying to the very extremes of the cavernous temple, "standing here . . ."

"And?"

"I—I can't remember . . ."

Sam recognized the look on her face. She had the déjà vu feeling again but it was all too fleeting. She was trying to remember something that she knew she'd experienced before but it was just too intangible.

"I don't mean to pressure you, but you'd better remember something soon," Sam said, motioning to the main doors at the other end of the dome. Outside, flashes of gunfire could be heard getting louder, now mingling with the sounds of sirens. Gabriella was silent, and Sam went about feeling around the interior, looking for a seam or a hinge that might reveal a concealed compartment, nearly tripping on the edge of the carpet as he made his way around the space.

"The floor—it was in the floor," Gabriella said.

*In the floor? The carpet? Well, that's certainly not an original feature . . .*

"*Under* the carpet," Sam and Gabriella said as one. They reached down together and tugged at the frayed corner of carpet until it tore free—

There, inset into the centre of the floor, was a brass crest. And in the centre of the crest, a shape, a star . . . just like the golden key around Sam's neck. He inserted it,

moving it around, trying to make it click in properly. After a few failed attempts at turning it, Gabriella took over. With her first twist—

*CLICK.*

**N**othing opened this time.

Instead, a disc of brass came free. The size of a small plate, it was circular with cogged teeth all around and markings around the edge.

"That's it!" Gabriella exclaimed.

"It's amazing," Sam said, holding the disc. "This was in your dream?"

"Yes! It *was!*" Gabriella's joyful shout reverberated around the room.

"OK," Sam said. "Now, listen carefully."

Gabriella grew serious once more and looked into his eyes. "Yes, Sam?"

"You're going to stay hidden here until Lora and her guys come to get you. Take these," Sam hurriedly took the book-like box out of his backpack and handed it to her, along with the brass disc. He tugged at the strap of his dream catcher, taking the golden key from the leather cord and placing it in her hand. "Go with the others, they'll keep you safe."

"No, Sam, *please.* Don't leave me alone," she begged.

"You'll be alright, I promise." Sam spoke slowly, recalling how calm Lora was in a crisis. "Remember, you can do this. Trust yourself, you know you'll be OK."

Gabriella nodded, and hugged him. "And you?"

Sam hesitated before standing up. "I have to lead Solaris away while you and the others escape."

The space was suddenly filled with the ominous sound of gigantic doors groaning open slowly. Sam walked away from the altar, stepping into the main hall under the dome.

There, standing in the doorway at the far side of the circular room, was an unmistakable silhouette.

Solaris.

"Just you and me, Sam . . ."

The metallic voice, inside here, was so loud that Sam had to cover his ears.

"Hand over what doesn't belong to you," he demanded.

Sam looked to his right. A side door. Maybe twenty metres away. He could crouch down, draw fire away from Gabriella, hope Solaris would miss . . .

Sam ran for it—

Fire streaked out, hitting the wall beyond his head as he ducked and dived. He rolled onto his feet and kept running, the second stream of fire hitting the ground behind him.

"Over here!"

Sam turned to see Gabriella standing at the altar, making Solaris hesitate just long enough for Sam to get to the door.

*Get down!* Sam willed her, seeing a ball of heat deflect off the curved marble wall near the altar as Gabriella ran for cover behind the ornate column to her left.

"Hey! Leave her alone!" Sam cried out. "I have what you want!"

Sam burst out of the door and was faced with an open run down a narrow and dark lane. With no side streets or diverging paths he'd be a sitting duck. Resisting the instinct to run, he waited, holding his breath.

Solaris came running out—

Sam caught him with an outstretched arm at his throat, but Solaris was too big for Sam to knock him off his feet.

Solaris retaliated immediately with a swinging blow, which Sam blocked. He twisted Solaris' arm and tried a jujitsu move and in the process felt something go *POP.* He realized Solaris' flame-thrower had well-concealed metal tubing that snaked around his wrist, which Sam had disconnected. It was leaking a thick liquid that smelled like gasoline. *Not so superhuman after all.*

*WHACK!*

Sam was knocked to the ground. He felt the force of a heavy boot in his stomach, and he rolled with the impact across the cold stone road. He tried to catch his breath. His vision blurred and he felt like he was about to slip out of consciousness. Through the blinding pain he could make out Solaris standing over him, trying to reconnect his flame weapon. So far, without success. *Good.*

*Splat, splat, splat—*

"Argh!" Sam spun up and off the ground, wiping the sticky fuel off his face.

"The key!" Solaris demanded, threatening with the flame-thrower at point-blank range.

Sam's hand instinctively moved to where he was used to the key hanging around his neck, before remembering he had given it to Gabriella.

"Or else what?"

Solaris said nothing.

"You won't kill me," Sam said. "You need me."

Before Solaris had a chance to react, Sam made a break for it.

Sam's heart beat loudly in his ears and he felt his chest running out of oxygen, his body starting to succumb to the night's stress and fatigue. He was desperate to get out of this open lane, with nowhere to turn off and nowhere to hide.

Solaris' footfalls behind—

Close.

Closer.

Closer still.

Sam ducked and spun in the same moment that Solaris made a move to tackle him. Carried by each other's momentum, arms locked, they rolled down the steep street, over an old sandstone retaining wall, crashing onto the ground nearly two metres below.

Sam was flat on his back, seeing stars.

Solaris was next to him, motionless, his hand clinging to Sam's pack, ripped clean off Sam's back in the tussle. Blood on a large rock near Solaris' head explained why he had not woken yet.

Sam dragged himself up and grabbed one of the straps to pull the backpack free. Hesitating slightly, heart in his mouth, Sam slowly reached down toward the concealed face of his enemy, ready to pull off his mask, but this one had no seams like the impostor's in New York.

*What am I expecting to see?*

Solaris twitched and began to stir.

*Don't push your luck, go!*

Sam turned and ran.

## EVA

Eva couldn't stop shaking. Lora put an arm around her. It was silent. No more firing from the Guardians, no yelling and screaming. No more Solaris. Just the monotonous two-tone sirens of Italian police vehicles rushing to the scene.

The new dawn was approaching and small shafts of light pierced the square between the narrow spaces of the surrounding buildings.

"Where's Sam gone?" Eva said.

"It's OK," Lora said, holding her.

The Guardians, now working with the authorities through their connections with the local law enforcement, still crowded around, their weapons ready for any threat that might resurface. Beyond them, in the grey light, security personnel were assessing the damage in the square and ushering away arriving onlookers and reporters.

"But what if Solaris took him?" Eva said, and started to cry.

"He'll be OK," Lora said. "Shh, it's OK."

Eva wiped away her tears.

Gabriella emerged from within the temple looking exhausted. She stood at the top of the stairs, still trembling with shock. Eva went over to her and gave her a hug.

The three of them stood silently together on the stairs, each trying to process the night's events.

"Come on, let's go," Lora said finally, her voice soothing and sure. "Sam is stronger than you think and he knows where he needs to go. We need to get you two back to the Academy, you're still not safe here."

Eva nodded. Her eyes scanned over the piazza one last time. Bits of broken stone and rubble from the fallen fountain were scattered across the square. Water still trickled out over the edge of the crushed fountain.

Gabriella looked at Eva, then followed her gaze. "Don't worry, there are plenty more such monuments in Rome."

Eva gave a little chuckle and wiped away a tear. With their Guardian escort, the three walked huddled together toward their waiting vehicles.

"You did well, we all did," Lora said to Eva and Gabriella. "Sam will be fine. Solaris would not dare harm him. He needs him just as much as we do. I'm sure Sam got away, he's not one of the last 13 for nothing."

Eva nodded. *But how can we be sure?* She had the unshakable feeling now that things would never be the same. Somewhere out there, her friend was in danger, putting himself right in the line of fire for her—for everyone.

## SAM

At the end of a small street where several narrow lanes converged, Sam came to a strip of cafés.

He hurried nervously along the rows of parked bikes and scooters, trying to blend in and go unnoticed by the early-morning café patrons inside. He slowed to a casual saunter, weighing his options. *How am I going to get out of here?* He crossed the road, a solution perhaps presenting itself.

*Mom never did let me ride a motorbike.* He grinned to himself, remembering the dirt bikes at Bill's uncle's farm, where they'd raced through muddy tracks and done jump tricks.

Before Sam was a row of scooters. He worked his way down, looking for one that he could perhaps . . . *yeah, maybe that one.*

He bent down to adjust his shoelace next to an old Vespa scooter with a kick start. It belched out a cloud of blue smoke as he wobbled into the thoroughfare, a young woman running out into the street shouting Italian obscenities as he drove out of reach.

A few minutes later he was weaving north, as quickly away from Solaris as the little engine would take him. *Bill would have loved this.* In his pocket, his phone rang. He pulled over to answer, the engine idling loudly.

"Lora?"

"Sam, it's Xavier!"

"Xavier?" Sam said.

"Yeah. Don't know . . . can hear . . . I'm . . . right?"

The crackly phone line and the fact that Xavier was somewhere incredibly noisy made it impossible to hear what he was trying to say. Sam killed the engine and pressed the phone tight to his ear.

"I can't hear you! Where are you?" Sam shouted into the phone.

". . . Ahmed . . . from Cairo . . . message . . . and it's . . ." Xavier's voice kept cutting out.

"I still can't hear you! I'll call you back," Sam said, unable to make any sense out of the few words he'd heard. He hung up and dialled Xavier's number. It went straight to voicemail. He tried again, with the same result.

Then Sam saw there was a text from Lora—

Eva and Gabriella with me. All OK. Solaris gone for now.

He typed in his reply.

Need to keep you all safe. Will contact once I know where I'm headed.

Sam put his phone back in his pocket and took off once

more, merging with the traffic, the cool early morning air on his face. As he got up to top speed, he thought of nothing but wanting to see Solaris and the Enterprise beaten for good. He'd won out twice now.

*Eleven Dreamers to go. How hard could it be?*

Sam swerved as a large black van veered in front of him, swearing loudly at the careless driver in some newly learned Italian. As the van slowed in front of him, he was forced to drop down to its speed and noticed the foreign licence plate. Another van pulled up to his left. The van squeezed him until he was almost over onto the shoulder of the road.

*What's going on? Surely Italian drivers can't be this bad!*

Next to him, the van's side doors slid open and Sam immediately recognized the wolf insignia on the uniforms of those inside. He was flooded with relief and began to smile.

*German Guardians . . . they're here to rescue me.*

Then they pulled out their weapons.